GAFFER

A novel of
Newfoundland

Kevin Major

Doubleday Canada Limited

For people of the new found land,
especially those of the Eastport Peninsula

Canadian Cataloguing in Publication Data

Major, Kevin, 1949–
    Gaffer

Hardcover ISBN 0-385-25667-1; Paperback ISBN 0-385-25729-5

I. Title.

PS8576.A523G33   1997   C813'.54   C97-930547-0

PR9199.3.M34G33   1997

Photo of shore scene by Kevin Major
Photo of astrolabe from *The Visual Dictionary of Ships and Sailing,* courtesy
    The National Maritime Museum, London
Cover design by Tania Craan
Text design by Heidy Lawrance Associates
Text photos by Kevin Major
Map from *Newfoundland: A Pictorial History*, Charles P. deVolpi: Longman
    Canada Limited, 1972
Printed and bound in the USA

Published in Canada by
Doubleday Canada Limited
105 Bond Street
Toronto, Ontario
M5B 1Y3

The author gratefully acknowledges the support of The Canada Council and The Newfoundland and Labrador Arts Council during the writing of this book.

Lyrics from "Let Me Fish Off Cape St. Mary's" by Otto Kelland.

BVG 10 9 8 7 6 5 4 3 2 1

Printed by Presso Antonio Zatta, Venice 1778

Also by the author

No Man's Land

"The Novels of Kevin Major"

http://www.newcomm.net/kmajor

Wind whines and whines the shingle,
The crazy pierstakes groan;
A senile sea numbers each single
Slimesilvered stone.

From whining wind and colder
Grey sea I wrap him warm
And touch his trembling fineboned shoulder
And boyish arm.

Around us fear, descending
Darkness of fear above
And in my heart how deep unending
Ache of love!

James Joyce
On the Beach at Fontana

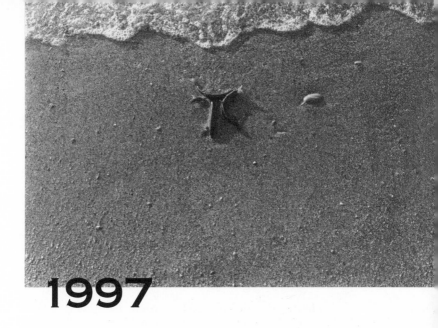

1997

He vowed he would never end up like them.

They ganged together at the edge of the bank, revving a hulk of rusted Ford, hanging out the windows. A wad of lunatics in the box, pounding more dents into the roof. Skidder, the scum, the head one, yelling down at him.

'Gaffer! What the fuck ya at now?'

He stood alone on the beach rocks, tattered track suit over his swim trunks. Stick in his hand, poking at pitted shards of wood lapped on shore the night before.

'Ship off! Morons.' Not looking up.

They laughed hysterically, slapped each other silly. Skidder ground the tires into the gravel, to the axles. The clump of hash-oil freaks heaving at the rear end of the truck, gone then in a final spit of dirt.

Gaffer would sneer for the time it took to pry apart another knot of debris.

He never found much—snarls of frayed rope, bits of salt-rotted plastic. Once a bottle. The likes of it he'd never seen before. And, dog to buried bones, he was back to the beach, firking at it again and again.

In the Gulch, one June morning, after the last of the Friday-night boozers had dragged himself home, Gaffer unsnagged from a scrap of fishnet what he claimed was the belt of a life jacket. Some dirt-faced youngster came scouring the place for beer bottles. Some snotnose chafing at his heels to show what he'd found.

Gaffer held it in the air, excitement taking grip of him. The kid scoffed at it, called him a psycho. Gaffer grabbed him by the scruff of the neck and drove him off. Told him to fly the frig to blue blazes.

At school Gaffer kept to himself, scrawling notes behind his textbooks, ignoring slime names whispered loud enough for him to hear. And the snarky excuses not to include him in the laughing rumble of their sex-talk. Even had he welcomed it, not one his age was of a mind to become his ally. Foul mouths jabbering on no end, and nothing-talk of dirtbikes and video games. He had no time for stupid idlers.

And for a good many adults he had less. Those that spewed off to strangers about him—the boy not yet born when his lone wolf of a father and the Yankee drill rig on which he worked were lost off the coast in a mad winter storm. Them waiting for the pangs of remorse it would unleash. And the hushed clamour for the details.

'Poor soul. Can't be right in the head,' he overheard once.

'Pity the poor young bugger, I do.'

He suspected as much. Wonder they didn't lump him in with Scuzz, the street-prowling halfwit who ranted on a mile a minute and never had the sense to wipe his drool.

'Give the devil hes due, poor Gaffer's not stunned.'

Nothing made him spitier. He'd have shag-all to do with any of them even if they were neighbours and what they were after was a few civil words.

Never in their souls to be merciless, they claimed they understood the boy. Let him go about the Cove as he chose. The next moment beating their gums in warning of the harm that would come his way, and dearly vowing, by the grace of the saints, he wouldn't bring trouble to any of their children.

They paid heed to him when he smiled and when he didn't. In the one breath they called him a keener; then proclaimed him moody, contrary as a cut dog, quick with sly expressions never to be trusted.

Better they spit their rebuke and he'd jump into the pit of an argument. Not their way. Them nor their blood before them. If nothing else on this Island, they got along with each other. How else to survive centuries on such a coast of barren rock?

It came as no surprise to any of them when for days Gaffer was nowhere to be seen. Neither hide nor hair of him. And some of them with half their day spent back and forth to the kitchen window. His mother would tell the ones brassy enough to ask that he wasn't himself, and recount symptoms of which none of them could understand a word.

Truth was he sat about in his uncle's deserted fishing shed, in the acrid scent of tar and oakum and salt-encrusted coils of manila. Days spent scrutinizing charts, creased and finger-blackened, memorizing whatever was to be found about the waters beyond the Cove. He'd go over and over them again until there was a steady whirl of headlands and shoals and sunkers circling his brain.

He loved the names—Shag Rocks, Cuckolds Point, Damnable Head, Damnable Neck—ringing with the alluring barbarism of the forbidden and the unknown. Some fiendish thrill in the way they rolled off his tongue. Would the namers have slurred them behind jagged stumps of teeth, hawked them out with their blackened spit? High sea rogues, greedily searching the coastline for codfish in numbers greater than their wily West Country masters had ever dreamed.

Gaffer's uncle had been the only one to accept his ways, though in recent months the man had no liking for his many questions, now that there was not a codfish to be had and not one sound reason to put gear in the water.

In the spring, when his uncle should have been fixing his nets, the boy showed up on the wharf every day after school, and stayed there by himself. He would fix his stare for the sparsest sign of activity about the place. Not so much as the old seadogs, who, angled against their walking sticks, used to spend their waking hours going from fishing shed to fishing shed. He scowled to think of any one of them in front of the TV soap operas with his missus.

On such days, the boy would be seen jumping ice pans out from shore. His mother warned him against it, but it was that or have his head rot in vexation. He'd leap from one to the next, to the next, until he'd landed on the most distant pan he knew would bear his weight. Several times a foot slipped into the slush and slob ice, but he never failed to haul it back and keep his balance. Steadied himself with the spike of a gaff, one he'd scraped clean of rust, from his uncle's fishing store. One his great-grandfather took aboard the bloodhound ships on his seal-hunting trips to the floes.

The old fellows looked out from their porches in amazement at the sureness of his step and decided on the name for him. Reminded them of the wiry nerve of their own youth. They smiled like they did at the thought of the sweet secret places of their women, when they were girls, before too much homemade bread and too many children got the better of them.

When Gaffer showed up at home one day soaked to the skin his mother held him rigid by the shoulders and told him it was something not to be doing ever again. The words stumbled from her mouth, for she had gripped thick muscle she never knew existed, and no longer had to look down to see into his eyes as she had done just months before.

He sloughed off her fretful patter.

'I'm not about to lose you,' she said.

'*He* would never want me to skulk away.'

Gaffer's stare stilled her tongue. She was lost for the words that should have come so easily.

When the ice melted and it hinted at being summer Gaffer waded into the water, it frigid still. He seemed not to notice, or care, that he had an audience.

Even the smartass Skidder would never brave such cold and, instead, stood with his mob on shore, blowing smoke rings, shouting that Gaffer was crazier than the fuckin' gulls, and squawking at him to prove it.

Until the time snow flared in his face he could be seen diving from rocks, submerged for endless minutes, breaking the surface in one slick motion, only to dive again seconds later.

Gaffer took to the water with a fervour adults angrily declared was unnatural. The ones who had never laid eyes on him ranted on the most, discounting claims he was strangely exhilarated and eager to have it consume him. The boy will catch his death, they decreed, and there was swift talk of neglect. 'Spends too much of her time in the club, wailing in that microphone.'

But no one could ever prove the water did him any harm, and they finally gave up saying it was so when they saw him outrun much older boys and hardly lose the rhythm of his breath.

Of those who watched him dive, there was one who stayed apart from all the rest. Came and went without a word to anyone. A stray whose hand rose once when he surfaced, signal to him? He dove, came to the surface closer to shore, but she had gone.

He had not known her face before. Some visitor, some relative, too chaste to have herself noticed for long? He went about his task, and hardly thought of her again.

On the day he learned his uncle would have to leave the Island he raced to find him. Came upon him staring out the doorway of his shed, at the saltwater as it lapped the wharf. The man knew the cod would never return inshore in numbers he could fish.

'Not right,' the boy spit out.

'We warned them. That bunch of greedy scoundrels would have us take the last one from the sea.'

His uncle knew the boy could not bear to see him go. Though he knew there was no choice.

'What's a fisherman to do when his boat is doomed to dry-rot?'

The man had a family who depended on his work and so all of them packed up to leave the Island where they were born and would have lived all their lives.

'Shed's yours, Gaff. You're the head one now.'

When their van pulled away there was not one of them inside it who looked back. The youngsters had begun already to squabble about when they would get to Wonderland and who would have guts enough to ride the Top Gun.

The van disappeared over the hill and there was nothing more said about it. The boy had his mother and grandmother. Now his only relations in the place.

The numbers of those his age dwindled and his mother was left to think that when he finished with school there would be no choice for him but to be gone off too.

His mother dreaded the day it would come to that. She tried to hold him to her in the evenings before it was time for bed. But he was beyond the age of anything more than a simple hug and a stolen kiss.

'I know there's nothing for you here,' she would start, but get no further before tears began to well.

He said nothing.

'What would your father have to say about it all?'

'He'd snarl and curse the bloody fools who got us in this godforsaken mess.'

She had to smile, his look reminding her of the man.

In those weeks since he had grown in stature to so resemble his father her mind had been more at ease than any time since the rig went down. There were times when she caught a glimpse of her son and it was as if the boy's father had never been lost. As much as she feared for the boy, she knew it only natural that he be set to take on the world, as he had always pictured his father to be on that awful night.

His grandmother bore no such sympathy.

'What, ya dear,' she burst out, 'leave us without a man in the house?'

She was a gabby beefbucket of a woman. The lard of her upper arms jangled when she walked; her ankles inflated her shoes. Her mighty beam pulled and twisted the seams of her cotton dress, its straps lost in the folds of flesh that were her shoulders.

She spent her waking hours in the kitchen. Baking constantly, it seemed. Mostly for church suppers or Legion dos. She had people believing she could cater to weddings single-handedly. There was no end to the cakes and tarts and puddings that rose from her oven, and no end to the praise she channelled her way.

'And I was thinking there'd be youngsters of yours running around the yard, their sweet little hands clutching yer nan's pork buns.'

Gaffer took to the stairs, though not before she had put a plate in his hand, with a warm cut of partridgeberry pie oozing across it.

The next spring he was forever at the shore. The hours he spent in the saltwater no longer passed as the antics of an adolescent boy, but left people thinking he had sure enough lost his wits, that it was only a matter of time before he would drown. There was great consternation among those who clustered together in view of him. They jabbered on and on and threatened to call the authorities on his gallivanting mother.

Gaffer paid no heed to their warnings, and submerged himself for longer and longer spans of time. Eventually they were at a loss to keep track of where his head cracked the surface, and felt foolish when they would spy him waist-deep, his hands raised in fists over his head.

Day after day he passed through saltwater until the briny fluid engulfed him, permeating his skin, its oxygen pulsating in time with his blood. He knifed his way through the water, skin hardened to sealeather, holding off the cold.

Skin the colour of dulse. In its darkest creases, blood purple. Dense grain, dense as hide.

When he wended his way home, his hair matted with salt, in thick clumps grazing his bare back, these clusters of people flinched at the sight of him. Threw their hands to their faces, moaned from deep down their lungs.

'Soak my wounds in briny waters,' he threw their way. 'Gawk no more. I bear witness to your shame.' His arms melded to his body. His piteous, sloshing gait, every reason to think he would veer into their path. And a face they could not abide—flattened so much his eyes bulged at them, lidless, with nostrils that flared, lips pressed inward in a fearsome strain.

'Gentle Redeemer,' they murmured. 'What has the world come to?'

'What, at all,' he chuckled, and gave them one last twisted stare.

When he had passed he let his face muscles rest and his features distend to what they had been before. That he could carry off such foolery caused a grin to curl across his lips.

At home he spent more and more time alone in his room. His mother and grandmother knew that to be the way of a boy changing to a man, though it worried them how little he spoke when they were together and how he seemed forever preoccupied with matters they knew nothing about. His mother saw even more in him that reminded her of his father, in stature and in his notion to pay no mind to what others said of him.

There were days he frightened her with the water noises from behind the bathroom door. When she rapped at the door to allay her fears that he was drowning in the tub, he yelled out that it was all her imagination, laughing that he was perfectly sane. She hardly knew if he was to be believed, but went away, wondering what would become of him.

'Trust me.'

'What's a mother to think?'

She had long ago come to see that he would never be like others his age, and had even come to take pride in his streak of independence. Its recent direction, however, caused her to grieve that her son would never have a life that would bring him any happiness. She found little comfort in knowing he embraced whatever he was after with faith and tenacity while others his age slouched about in idleness.

'Your son, the malcontent,' he said, smiling. 'Whatever becomes of me you'll know I did it for good reason.'

She glared at him, not willing to be anything but stiff in her resolve to keep him from harm.

His grandmother prayed for him every night and pulled him unabashedly to her mountainous bosom and held him there as if it were impossible to defy a love so strong. With copious sweat he was able to surface and regain his breath. He tried to smile like he did when he was a child, blurting out that he would never forget how much she cared for him.

'Gentle Saviour, spare me to see you a grown man, with a wife to bake for you and keep clothes on your back, and a civil tongue in her mouth.'

Gaffer, who could think of no girl he knew transforming into such a woman, passed it off. Yet he knew he would have to set her mind at ease. 'Blessed are the heavy-laden,' he said. 'For they shall find rest.'

The words, so familiar to her, and coming from his own lips, brought tears to her eyes. She held out her fat arms and clasped him vise-like to a bosom swelling with pride.

He managed to extract himself again. Gone then he was to recover. Content, at least, in knowing that he had been the grandson that she needed.

His mother remained his concern. He knew of no way to quiet her fears. He slipped down the stairs later at night and found her alone at the kitchen table, sipping a remedy of pungent tea. He could hold forth no hope that he could ever be the son she would need.

'But you are in my heart wherever I go.'

She ignored the earnestness in his voice. 'Your stubborn streak I can abide, but your father's fool-hardiness I never wanted to see in you.'

'What would you have me do—sit in front of the television and hear government suits rant on about what is wrong with this place? The gall. Them with no mind to listen when the answers were all around us.'

It gave her no comfort. He wrapped an arm around her shoulder and he talked of the first time she took him to the beach, a child hardly walking.

'Couldn't think it,' she said. 'Possessed you were. Screamed blue murder to stay in the water.'

The fear that had gripped her seemed to take hold again. She shivered at the touch of his arm, and could not believe it was the son she had nurtured all those years.

The boy is not well, she resolved. He could not help but smile at her persistence, for he knew nothing would make her see the futility of her notions. He played her game, feigning the comforted and peaceable offspring that she could hold to her.

That night she came into his room and kissed him goodnight. She whispered words she had whispered when she rocked him for the endless nights when he was an infant.

At the first light of dawn he was gone, not knowing if he would ever return.

As the sun's rays flickered at the distant edge of the sea, he stood on shore lathering his bare self with the seal fat that had rendered to oil in his uncle's shed. A thick rancid grease to stave off the cold and make supple his leather skin. He worked it into every crease and hollow, even about his head, spitting it away when it touched his lips. Ran what seeped between his fingers through his hair, slicking it black and shiny, flat to his head. He donned trunks to streamline him. Stood, hands overhead sharpened to an arrow, tautly poised upon a rock, the carved youth of a man aimed toward the swirl of the highest tide.

Behind him stood wharves and stages of a people who had claimed this Island five hundred years before, whose houses had given a dozen generations of toilers for the sea, whose numbers now sank like an anchor rusted from its chain.

His lungs filled to bursting, emptied to the last molecule, and again and again, each time more rapidly than before, his nostrils broadening to the strain that seemed desperate for something else; the same time his cheeks collapsed, his eyes set forward, open and rigid, intense on the foam before him. His toes curled the jagged rock.

He sprang, a lance like that of birch and hide and flint cast by the ancient peoples who came to that shore. He clove the saltwater and the saltwater closed over him, without trace of entry save a rainbow-thin film of oil.

The realm below took him in as one of their own. He knifed a course through clumps of shoreline kelp, fought off the pull of tide, the brush of detritus swirling from the bottom. He broke clear, water streaming past skinfolds of his neck thick now with blood vessels, sucking oxygen that rejuvenated the pump of a splendid specimen of heart.

It was his heart that set him free into all the depths of brine, so when he swam, wild and loose and with a showman's twist of his leg, he rejoiced like a fingerling burst free from its egg.

He thrust through the water, fuelled by the blast of new respiration, showing the bluster of grilse, fearlessness of young shark, tenacity infused by the hammer of injustice.

'Sweet salvation!' he intoned, breaking the surface, arching with great panache back into the water. Dolphin almost, in expectation of applause.

At the sight of him two poachers fell flat to the

ribs of their boat. 'Blessed Saviour!' And a thunderous Hail Mary, full of grace, in unison.

'Was it not the boy?' cried one.

'Devilfish,' proclaimed the other, and both streaked to shore to spread the word.

Below the surface, far from their piercing, receding eyes, he laughed, slap laugh of limb against his body, his intensity a raw current through the water, the sheer thrill of surging free through a new universe. He darted about, his every move confirmation that impassioned scheme had become his life.

His commotion parted schools of capelin. He took immense joy at the sight of the silver fish. Swerved and chased after them. They darted one way, then another in the half light near the surface. They were nothing to the size of those that spawned in the June tides when he was a youngster, nothing near it, or in numbers, either.

Capelin were the fish of his happiest days, when they swelled on shore to cast eggs and milt onto the sand, and he would teeter atop the sponge barefoot and have it ooze about his ankles, and tumble into it, clutching great globs to fling at bawling little playmates in their sundresses.

Capelin marked the beginnings of his summers; their coming to shore set the rhythm of his seasons. He rejoiced at the flick and tumble of thousands of creatures upon the beach. He rolled and waded among them, their tails brushing his baby flesh to send him into fits of squealing. Once he rose up from the surf with one caught between his teeth, its wriggling tail to one side of his mouth, its head to the other.

His uncle would fling the circle of a castnet over the schools of capelin, yanking it tight, dragging it dense to shore to release them, quivering madly, into a bucket as tall as the child. The capelin spilled over the sides onto the sand, all about the feet of the laughing boy, who plopped down in the midst of them, trying to clutch some, only to have them squirm and slime through his hands.

He loved the look of them drying in his uncle's backyard—hundreds spread across wire mesh, hundreds more hanging from narrow strips of wood, hooked through their fish eyes on headless nails. The first day's sun would scab the outer skin, but a week might pass before they had dried and shrivelled through enough that they could be gathered in. Some sampled, and all the rest packed in freezers, brought out as a treat during the long nights of winter.

And Saturdays in the woods there were, sitting about on boughs in the snow, an open fire cracking hot below a tin can of boiling tea, his uncle roasting dried capelin at the end of a sharpened stick. His mother would not eat the whole of a capelin, but the boy did, head and all, and relished every morsel of it.

Your father's son, his mother would call him, and no doubt about that, ya dear, his grandmother would say. The boy mused, took uncanny satisfaction in it.

The memory sent him plunging deeper through the water, testing his endurance. He dove through the capelin schools, dazed by the sight of them, the thinness of the wave of them, the mindtwist of an optical illusion.

He dove to where his rigid body drifted back and forth between the certainty of light filtering from above to the deepening green pitch below. The sway of it mesmerized him—the mother's pleas from the shoreline cliffs, the aching mystery beyond the shores, dragging him first in one direction, now the opposite.

He kicked loose from the tangle, stroking vigorously free of the shorefast, headlong out to sea, far and away from the land that had held him by birthright.

He drifted upward and broke the surface just as he was about to round the headland. His head bobbed about the water. He looked back through the sea splash to the Cove. The sight strickened him, how the sun glinted off white saltboxes growing out of the rocks, indifferent to the ways of the world.

They had risen there when these waters swarmed with cod. Not one had he now encountered. Was there any hope for the bustle of boats about the harbour, the hum of work up and down the shore; was he to think history would never again make time on this coast?

He turned away, in scorn at the thoughts of some that such a raw face of rock was no place for a sane person. Better to drag it out to the sea, sink it and be done with it, the cur had said. The boy heaved at such guff. Let the pigfaces root their newspaper swill in their own backyards.

The boy did not look back. He rounded Cuckolds Point and headed to the open ocean, passing the Damnables, where in summertime lived only goats. He skimmed the surface long enough to see one look up from chewing thistles, eyeing him. He thought he could see his ribs.

'You had better days in the past, me bucko.' The boy laughed, a sardonic, seafarer's laugh. He was surprised at the saltiness of his voice. 'That you did,' he said, just to hear it again.

The goat continued the sway of his jaw, as if to say he'd heard it all before. When the boy sprayed a mouthful of saltwater in his direction, and curved and finned and danced across the surface then did the goat take notice.

'Name's Buckley,' said the goat. 'Been on this headland for centuries, lad. Seen stranger sights than you pass by.'

'That you have, bearded one.'

'Most of them come and go and never come back. Got what they want. Or what they deserve. A scattered few souls sticks it out. Renegades from reality some calls 'em. I don't think so. I wouldn't be here if that was the case.'

'They were happy enough, given a fair chance.'

'World's not fair, there's the fetter. Never was, not for me to know.'

'Not gonna change now,' the boy moaned in sarcasm. He dove through the waves. 'Chaw away. Keep them eyes sharp.'

'Knew your father,' pronounced the goat. 'Saw what he was after. Headstrong he was, too.'

The echo reached the boy just as he flicked himself below the surface.

1995

Buckley's words stayed with him, pushed him on, pressed at his heart, all the while him escaping the sight of land, blur through the water just below the surface.

He struck out, no distractions now, tin fish blown broadsides from a frigate.

Rakish young gulls and ticklaces, starved for fish guts, trailed him in a squawking tantrum of curiosity. Never saw the like of his speed. Never witnessed such a blade of creature through the water. What were they to make of this saltwater pup?

They circled his wake. With irksome, ugly cries headed back to shore. Gaffer was gone, to the sea bottom, where a backward glance was no temptation, where distance was not a measure between points of land.

He pressed on, weaving through the undersea. Boyfish striking a new world.

Skimmed past the bottom dwellers, the scattered clams and brittle stars, the sluggish shelled and spiny beasts holed up in the mud. The odd few fishes, some flattened to the bottom, most hardly to be noticed. Grey sole, plaice, flounder, turbot.

Gaffer's brain had long soaked with fish sense— manoeuvre through temperature change, avoid the lurk and sting of marauders desperate to escape the fate of their fellows. With a single-minded clench of conviction he set course. It drew him like a sunken hull draws hope, long after hope should have passed away.

The hope lulled him, only to be dashed by thoughts of his father swollen to a gutknot of contradictions. Where there were no answers, only fury at greed outweighing the lives of brave young men.

It drove an unswerving need to get there, to see for himself.

But in the black of unsettled night the great sweep of greed was upon him!

He had no warning. Behind him—a gaping huge mouth of net. Its lower jaw scraping the ocean floor in a billow of sediment. Mammoth predator chasing down the hapless ocean lodger, its width and breath sucking everything in its path into a giant swell of mesh. Scraping raw the ocean floor.

Gaffer made a dart for it, but the thick twist of rope caught his underbelly and sent him reeling into the net. Tumbled smack against a teeming wall of flatfish and crustaceans.

He sank into the wriggling slimy mass; the knife-edge fin of one, the claw of another scraped him, pricked him. Barbs and horny spikes scored his leather skin; vile slub smeared him end to end. Clogging every orifice. He twisted and flailed his limbs, to thrust himself clear of the wretched snarl, in vain, for more creatures swept in, flattening him into the mass.

The jaw of net yanked tight, a thick, ravenous noose. The strangling kink dragged clear of the bottom, swerving upward through the water. Gaffer slithered his way through the hoard, clawed passage to the top of the heap, only to be wedged against the twisted braid of net. He gripped the cord, striking two layers of mesh. Never a prayer of getting free. Never a hope of escaping the scourge of trap laid for the smallest of his kind.

Black gave way to a sickly half light. The net slammed against a lip of rusted iron. The gutload of sea life jolted to a stop. Gaffer bobbed in the splash between water and air, seas smacking the bloated bag against the stern hole of a ship.

Up from the water came the spoils, steel cable winched at a crawl, the bag jerking up the shaft into the ungodly glare of a floodlit deck. Gaffer, blinded, his flesh rubbed raw against the twist and knot of the mesh, could tell nothing of his captors, save the flash of fluorescence from their orange gear, their scramble to secure the load.

The night air was rife with the shouts and grunts

of burly, hooded men. They circled the net, jabbing it with the heels of their boots, as if to drive it further into submission. Seals beating their hands together to keep warm. They barked their pleasure, smoke from black tobacco flaring out with the words, the fag stumps never leaving their lips. The sea had delivered them their wage. And a damn sorry man it would be who would have it any other way.

Air drove out the last spurt of saltwater from Gaffer's chest. The boy knew only the quake of coughing, the squirm of his limbs trying to stretch. He lay splayed atop a quavering heap, its seablood sucked by gravity down the shaft and back into the sea.

Life drained from the mass, a cold tonnage dredged up on deck. The men lay in wait for the cable to slack, signal that the lockjaw net would split abroad.

Gaffer spewed forth, in a slithering, fetal curl. Mucilaginous clump of boy, wrinkled, flesh imprinted with the criss-cross of the net. He skimmed the slimy deck, slamming to a stop against a glaring green hulk of rope. Its coarse nylon ridges scraped the knobby length of his backbone. He moaned angrily.

The men sprang back at the sight of him. Could not believe their cock-eyed vision. What abyssal demon, what fathomless mutant had cast itself on them?

Gaffer slowly stretched to full measure, eons unfolding before their eyes, fish rising on two feet from the quagmire, a slub-smothered amphibian in human guise. His flesh glistened in the cold white glare of the floodlights.

A fellow grabbed a boat hook. Waved its steel tip in a torrent of snarling curses. Jumped to a sudden stop before him, boat hook poised at the level of his chest. Gaffer stiffened. His fingers curled in ire.

He clawed the slub away from his eyes, had it crawl down his cheeks, drop off his face. He flattened his hair to his skull. His hands drove a path from his throat, down his chest, down his thighs, flung stiff-armed away from his body in a splattering heave of fish mucus.

An edge of bloodied yellow muck caught the fellow's eyes.

He dropped the hook. Swerved away. 'Fuckin'
swine!' he yelled, dragging a sleeve across his eyes.
'Damned heathen bastard!'

Their curses slashed the night air, guttural cross-
fire lashing him. Gaffer stood iron-chested against
it all.

'*Imbécil!*'

'*Tolo!*'

'*Maudit salaud!*'

'Bloody savage!'

Damn curse on their catch, they called him. What
right had he to interfere with a decent man slaving to
make a decent wage?

'Lucifer's own!'

And made for him, a contemptuous mob.

The boy leapt away from them. Landed on a
clump of gear. His deftness a scent that sickened
them, retching their collective spite. They roared, pack
of demented beasts, swerved and charged him again.

He sprang to a railing, eyes blazing, in the full
flare of the floodlights. 'Not yours to pillage,' he lashed
at them. 'You'll scrape and scour till the last one is

frozen in your hole. Your owners glory in their dis-
grace! And then what will your people have on their
plates?'

They took no heed, and cursed his gall. They
made for him again.

'Get back, scoundrels! Get back to the waters that
wash empty on your own damn shores. We've turned
blind eye to your thievery long enough.'

'*Vá para o inferno!*'

'*Vete a la mierda!*'

'We are not the ones!'

'*Vive les mers libres!*'

Gaffer spit at their nonsense.

They lunged at him! Defy their honour—he would
not! An iron pipe slammed the iron railing inches
from his feet. Rattled him to his core.

'Shameless fools!'

Brandished the iron pipe again they did, with
rabid viciousness. He sprang away. Backwards he
soared, a flying fish of a man, up and over the side,
a defiant arch of escape. Into the froth of black water.
Back to the sea from whence he'd been snagged.

The ruffians on deck howled in surly pleasure at the fate of one who dared to think them anyone but masters of the deep. They swung a light on him and gawked at the water swallowing him up. Cheered at the thought they were rid of the damned foreigner and his claptrap.

They took to their true task—clearing the catch to the freezers below, making way for another fling of the net.

1999

Gaffer sank below the waves, drifting down without turn of a limb.

Limbs wrenched, raw and bruised. Skin torn open to the ocean's salts.

He withstood the pain, knowing it would cleanse and mend them. He fell freely through the depths, to restore what they had maimed.

His senses sharpened. No renegades would close in on him again.

He fought off the curl and stiffness of his healing skin. He played at fish games—took to their schools and took nourishment from their scraps. In holes and caves he lurked about. There found his refuge, and rested more.

He drifted near the surface, drawn back by the sun's familiar rays. He hung there. Bare, impatient sinew of youth, wanting still to prove itself. Not able to withstand the promise of the homeward tide.

Gaffer washed up on the shore in the early hours of morning. The water pushed him up and dragged him back, each time less so, until he lay a motionless clump atop the sand.

Soft sputtering as water receded and breath returned to him. He lay still. Debris, a despondent mound, not willingly back to shore, with no energy to take to the sea. He sank into sleep.

The poke of a stick against his shoulder blade broke his rest. Gaffer lifted his head. Sluggard, sand caked to the side of him. His teeth ground the grit that clogged his mouth.

'Knew it had to be you.'

He swiped at the damn stick. Saw the sun-dark legs of a girl sitting near him. His eyes turned slowly upward. Past a chemise, wet, clinging to her, the colour of onion skins. He stopped at her face and its edge of a smile. A brush of downy hair glazed her head, a small silver ring pierced one ear. Eyes, deep-set blue, seeing all. The girl who stood alone on the bank and watched his dives.

'Been on the lookout for you.'

Startled by her coarse, impudent tone. 'You?' he scoffed.

'Not exactly normal beachcombing fare, you're not.'

His annoyance turned to a scowl.

'Withstood a lot, by the look of your bruises.'

She reached out to touch his back, but he recoiled and almost hissed at her.

'I brought a jar of salve.' She jerked her eyes toward a brin pouch hanging at her side.

He glared at her.

'Bullheaded. Course, I expected no better.'

'Who are you?' he spit.

'There's nobody who should have anything to do with you? Is that it? Content to lie here, then, some sodden pitiful wretch?'

Cursed her up and down. 'Get away. Who needs you!'

She stood up. The early-morning sun caught her earring. Match for the brooding fire in her eyes. 'Someone will.'

She walked off.

'I had a father,' she muttered, half turning back. 'Once, I had a father.'

He peered up to follow her walk down the length of the beach. She climbed the rocks at its end and disappeared.

The unrest she had brought hung over him. Gradually he rose up from the sand. Washed himself in the ocean.

He made his way, with crude and hasty gait, toward his uncle's fishing shed. Curtains in each house he passed were pulled aside. Drawing there a bunch of gawkers for his trek.

The shed became his place of convalescence, his

refuge. The smells his oxygen, the sights a balm for his wounds. He rigged up a hammock with fishnet, cushioned it with oilcloth. He ate hardtack and drank from dirty brown bottles of homebrew. He oiled pulleys and strung them with rope, apparatus to force the strength back to his limbs.

He dug through his uncle's crate of battered books, craving solace in the deeds of those who had come to shore before him.

In the tangled sensuousness of half sleep, he thought of the girl, her bare legs rubbing each other. The sand clinging to her thighs.

Her image filled his head. Stirred his blood. He drove it back. He would have nothing to do with her. Out for something, she was. Too quick with her gypsy tongue.

He emerged from the shed, as sound in body and mind as ever he was. Tramped through the village, pallor of defiance about him. A seasoned scowl for the nosy onlookers.

He found his way home, with the expectation of some oven-sweet aroma wafting from the kitchen.

Was met instead by the caustic cut of disinfectant. His nerves cramped. Expected a rush of open arms; alone he was at the bottom of the stairs.

Eventually he lumbered up the stairs, caught another scent. Liniment, chased it to his grandmother's room. He entered and saw her drop a tabloid paper to the floor.

She lay in a great heap aboard the double bed. Her arms stacked one atop the other across her sprawling chest. She looked as if she was never to rise again.

'Gaffer,' she whimpered. 'You've come to rescue me from the jaws of paralysis, my sweet.'

'Nan…'

'Hard to fathom, I know, my sweet.'

Gaffer wandered closer, only to have her snare his head and hold it to her lips. Her breath smelled of peppermint knobs, her hair emitted the acid fumes of a packaged perm.

She bounced her open hand lightly against the mass of tiny curls. 'Just 'cause the legs give out on me, no reason not to keep decent. Lookin' fine yourself, Gaffer. Change did you reams o' good.'

'What's the matter, Nan?'

'The gout, that was the start of it, ya dear. Doctor says to keep off the feet. And the church's 125th anniversary coming up, too. They had me down for dinner rolls and bakeapple tarts. Now they'll have to get something store-bought, I dare say.'

'Someone will be there to take up the slack.'

'Like to think so, I would. Lord only knows what'll come of it all. Mostly the old crowd, that's all what's left now. They'll do their best. Got to put your trust in people, I s'pose. Not the same now as doing it yerself.'

Imagined her, he did, wheeled into the kitchen of the church hall on the anniversary night, parked before the stoves, and left to flail her flabby arms about in a frightful chorus of directions.

A glaring sign something had come over him. Never had his grandmother unearthed pity in him before. Who'd have imagined such a thing?

Overcome he was by the urge to hoist her out of bed and set her in motion himself. How was it any-thing but damned depressing to see her lying there,

a gelatinous mass of uncertainty, growing more contrary by the minute. Never was it how he pictured
his grandmother growing old.

'Gaffie, do me a favour and bring up a TV. Just
so's I'll have something to take me mind off it,
you know. You can put it right there where you
be now.'

'No.'

'Gaffie?'

'Nan! What, in the name of God and ...'

She didn't know what to make of such an out-
burst from her darling boy. Blood rushed to her face
and she grieved to think him so out of sorts. 'You
can do that much for your dear old nan...'

Her words trailed away, for he was out the door
and down the stairs.

He sat at the kitchen table, eyes scanning the
kitchen for the least sign of her former self. Every
bowl and utensil clean and in its place. Not so much
as a wisp of flour on the countertop.

'Your nan is not as young as she used to be.'

His mother's voice, from the living room.

He stood up. Made his way inside. Saw first her smile, constricted smile, her sharpest features even sharper. The flick of a cigarette in her outstretched hand.

Yet his heart went straight out to her. They embraced under her shroud of smoke.

'Couldn't help it,' she said. 'Nerves were gone. Damned depressing around this place. Getting so there's nothing but grey hair and walking canes. They closed the school. Yanked what kids were left aboard the bus for two hours a day.'

'Nobody stood up to them?'

'Tired of it.'

He did not hide his disappointment.

She took a draw on her cigarette. Stubbed it out with the smoke rising in a cloud from her mouth.

'And you vowed there'd never be another one touch your lips.'

She shrugged. Piled atop his disappointment. Quick to add, 'It wasn't you, Gaffer. I knew you'd be back.'

He sat down and stared at her. Her hair streaked fire red, longer than it had ever been. For the first time in her eyes a glaze of loneliness.

'Time goes on, Gaffer. You're making your own way in the world.'

An acceptance his mother had never shown before.

'You miss him still?' he said.

'What's important for any of us,' she said, 'but our own peace of mind.'

They hugged each other.

'You're safe? You are, are you, Gaffer?'

She held his head in front of her and looked into his eyes. 'Couldn't hold you back. Couldn't do it when you were a child. Never do it now.'

He knew that of all he held close to him there was nothing more faithful than the love of his mother.

'I do what I have to,' he said to her, holding her hand. 'You the same.'

He kissed her on the cheek and quietly left the house.

He walked down the path. A man he did not recognize went past him, on his way into the house. Gaffer watched from a distance. Saw his mother greet the fellow at the front door.

She planted a kiss on his cheek. The door closed behind them and Gaffer stood staring.

He shut the gate and walked on.

He walked the village. But there was no comfort to be had. Curtainless houses and flower beds thick with grass. Rotting fences fouling property lines that had been so sacred. Half-starved cats and dogs snaking the overgrown paths between the houses.

The only one to seek him out was Skidder's mutt, a lump the size of an orange beneath the skin of its neck.

'Where's Skidder?' Not that Gaffer cared. Wanted only to see the reaction of the dog.

The mutt whined and veered closer to his heels.

Farther along Gaffer came across an old man, sitting outside in a front-porch chair. The sun beat against the dull white clapboard. The paint it scaled would not be replaced, with no sons around to help.

Who all had mortgages on the mainland. Whose grandsons, when they did come to visit, never understood a word he said.

He showed no wariness around Gaffer. Senile, no recollection of such a fellow? No longer cared?

Gaffer stopped outside his gate. The old man leaned forward in his chair and sized him up with an obstinate stare. A trace of a smile seen through twitching lips.

'Got guts, you have. Nothin' fer you on the mainland?' He coughed and spit into a handkerchief. He hardly seemed to have the lungs for such ardent talk.

Gaffer shook his head.

'Won't see neither one o' mine back 'ere no more. Both of 'em got jobs in a factory what makes fridges. I said, freeze yer arses off at dat, you will.'

A loud guffaw, enough to bring the slippered shuffle of his wife, wiping her hands in her apron. 'Whas ya at, Herb?' She caught sight of Gaffer. 'Alzheimer's,' she mouthed. She turned to her husband. 'Have a good laugh for yourself. You needs it.' She wiped his mouth with the end of her apron and shuffled back into the house.

'Alzheimer's, me arse,' the old fellow snapped, hauling the back of his hand across his mouth.

'You take care of yourself, now,' Gaffer called to him. 'This place wouldn't be the same without you.'

'You can say that again, crackie.' And laughed so loud he snorted.

'Herb!' his wife yelled. 'Be quiet, fer God and heaven's sake. You'll wake the dead.'

'They needs to be woke if you ask me. Course, they'd take one look at this place and over they'd roll again and haul the dirt back on derselves.'

Gaffer hung his hand in the air to the old fellow till he was gone far past his place.

A calm and cloudless day, kind of day that had always seen a steady stream of pickups between home and the saltwater. Overloaded with impatient, restless fishermen.

Tourists was what he came across, snarled in the romance of the place. A glut of lenses, gorging on every weather-pitted shed. Shutters jumping to rapid fire at the sight of those marked least by human hand. They noticed Gaffer and their eyes lit with possibilities.

One stealthy twig of a mainlander approached him with an offer of money in his hand if he would pose in front of an abandoned car.

'The dog, too, for good measure. Get him to turn sideways if you could.'

Gaffer glowered his way.

'You could use the bucks, I'm sure. Past the stage of hand-outs, aren't you now? You want to work for what you get. Only right.'

Gaffer flared at him, hound at the carcass of a flea-ridden cat. Walked away without a word. Skidder's mutt yelped and hobbled off in his own direction.

'Can't live in the past,' the fellow called after him. 'Can't ride a wave that's already crashed to shore.'

Gaffer heard more clicks of the camera. Made friggin' sure it caught the fist hanging down his side.

Found his way to the grassy bank that overlooked the beach, spot where the gawkers had followed his practice dives. He sat on its edge and surveyed the sea. Scrutinized the pitch of the soaring gulls. Swept his eyes slowly across the glint of water in hopes of detecting what was going on below. In one spot he noticed the change of colour. Saw it go flat in a way that made him suspect it was a whale.

He shed his shirt and lay atop it on his stomach. The sun his consolation. It warmed him to his bones. The tightness of his healing cuts eased off and he was left with a gentle throb along his spine. His eyes closed.

The sensation spread, massaging his worn flesh. Sweet, sweet rhythm that sent him drifting away, spirit drifting from the land.

He woke with a start. Opened his eyes to the glare of the sun, but could see the outline of a hand in midair, withdrawing to the side of her. Had it been the touch of her fingers along his skin? The lithesome rhythm of her palm?

And what of the stir of blood between his thighs? He sat up and hastily pulled on his shirt.

'You follow me. Why? Some oddity, is it, some diversion?'

'Hardly that.'

'What, then?'

'The fierceness of will I have not seen, for so long a time. That briny adrenalin coursing your veins.' She paused. 'Clogging your emotion.'

Gaffer sneered at her. 'Rather me spineless, would you? Like so much fish guts, for the gulls to shred? You and your female guile.'

She laughed out loud. 'Me, out to lure you off course?' And laughed again. 'You have it wrong. By far you have.'

'What, then?' he snapped, raging at her stupid laugh.

'Have you no time for anything but your anger?'

'For you?'

'And that is so peculiar, is it?'

'You could be the devil's own for all I know.'

'You care to find out even less.'

She swept away from him, with such haste that the sand from her naked feet flew in his face.

He yelled her way, 'Play the wounded bird. You know no better.'

He would give it no more thought. A senseless distraction. Rid his head of it he would.

She turned back. 'Gaffer,' she called. 'You be careful.'

Against his will he watched her fade into the distance. What was he to make of such a one? No girl had shown anything but snide indifference to his ways.

He sank back onto the ground.

Suddenly, a limousine, aquamarine, cut his line of sight. A thick block of fellow struggled from its seat. His sunglassed mate slithered out behind him and to his side.

Together they launched themselves along the bank. His shirt a riot of fleurs-de-lis, her hair an eagle's nest of blond debris. Her high heels veered toward the bank, a look-see before snuggling tighter to her mate.

'Who owns this land, *mon ami?*'

'It's not for sale.'

They chuckled. '*Sacre bleu,* but it's so far away from everything. Are you for real? Surely, it has no value. As it is.'

'As it is or not, it's not for sale.'

'Has potential, *mon ami*. Strike a deal, and in fifty, sixty, sixty-five years there could be flowing a handsome profit. Like a waterfall, yes, siree, *mon ami*.'

His mate purred approvingly.

'We work to deliver *the opportunity,* to the right people. And the right people will be all ears about this one. Yes, siree, jiminy fucking crickets!'

'Get out of here!' Gaffer screamed, so loud it recoiled from the hills.

The fellow narrowed his eyes. Grinned. Broadened his shoulders. Peered at Gaffer, raised a finger to him. '*Mon ami,* obviously you lack the spirit of the entrepreneur.' He shook his head. 'Get with it, *tout de suite.*' And laughed uproariously.

'Get back where you came from!'

The pair strutted to the car and drove away.

Only to stop at the first house with any sign of life.

Gaffer turned to the ocean. He ran down the bank to the water. Vehemently, he splashed the brine into his face, alerting his neurons of more to come.

He stripped to his trunks. Looked behind him. The bank deserted. Not the girl, no sign of anyone.

The wind rose, out of the northeast. A chilling wind. Toughened his will.

Plunged him into the sea. A torrent of energy. Locked in his head the far-off mooring, and its eighty-four souls soon rising up to confront the turmoil of a savage sea.

1982

He broke the surface
in the dead of night,
but a fleck at the
foot of a massive beast of an oil rig, towering more
than twenty stories above him. Looked hardly to be
of this planet, its searing floodlights shooting through
a grid of crane and derrick. From submerged pon-
toons rose eight elephantine legs, and, from these,
cable latched to chain latched to anchors snagged
the colossus to the ocean floor.

Gaffer spied up one leg the web of ladders

and catwalk that could get him to the deck. He swam for it, mindful that the water's lap did not smack him senseless against the brutish column wall.

He grabbed a rung and hauled his body tight. Clung to the metal treads, amphibious pup in the heaving surf. Sputtered and hawked and spit back the brine, rested till air drew easy into his chest.

Slowly he began his climb, one hand stretched past the other, draining clear of the night-black swirl of spume. Rung after rung, a sea-slug up the sheer of godless cliff.

He felt a backward tilt, and each step swelled the strain. Some hundred feet above the keel he dragged body and bones onto a catwalk and collapsed.

An exhausted mound that slowly rose again. Handrail for his guide, he shifted his carcass to the ladder whose peak would bring an end to his climb.

Gaffer came upon a porthole. Saw his first sign of life. Through the dulled, pitted chunk of glass he beheld a pair of men before a board of lights and switches. Mites in the monster's brain.

He left them to their game and resumed his climb. Peered not up nor down. Shut his eyes and found a rhythm in arms and legs—reach, hold, lock his grip, upward go. Up, up, crawl, steady, crawling, scaling, ever closer to the catwalk that rimmed an edge just below the deck.

He lay stretched along the catwalk, figure prone in the blessed night, sucking back his strength. For a while he slept. When he rose to his feet it was dark still, though above him glowed the ledge, the destination. He crawled from the underbelly, up the last few rungs. His head inched to just above the lowest pipe of railing.

The air blew rank with oil and grease and drilling mud. He slithered forth, concealed by a maze of storage tanks and pipe lengths, the rigid thrust of cable and cranes. He heard no voices, detected only a muffled clamour from the drill floor.

He lay in wait. The bundle of pictures and letters from his mother's dresser drawer had taught him well the layout of the rig. His brain fixed with the route to take in search of him.

This night, the night before the seas began to howl, his father would be sleeping. He set out for quarters below the helicopter deck, dodging from one spot to the next.

A blinding shaft of light. Behind it the scourge of Yankee bluster. 'Y'all tryin' to scare me. Us Louisiana boys don't scare so easy.'

Gaffer escaped and held taut in the dark. He could see the eyes sunk inside the hood of a day-glo heap of parka.

'Boy! Swamp dog. Newf. Show that face and you're breathin' crude.'

Gaffer flared. He emerged, defiant in his near-nakedness, in full view of the hawkish eyes. Scared the hell out of the Southerner. Sent him scampering to declare he had seen some hell-bound spook. Raved on that his mammy sure as hell knew of mud-sucking devilskins and such lurking in the bayou.

Gaffer raced on—slid past slabs of metal doors, down dim passageways, past numbers, more numbers, to the room he knew to be the one.

He slipped inside.

There was light enough across the bunk to see the peaceful mask of his face. The father in the photographs, asleep, but bearing still the wisp of daredevil youth.

Gaffer stared at him, and, stiff-faced, wept.

He sat at the side of the bed. He held back from rousing him, yet couldn't help but recite the sea-song words his mother could never bear to hear because they were her man's favourite.

'Take me back to that snug green cove / Where the seas roll up their thunder ...'

It broke his sleep.

'Father,' the young fellow said.

The man slowly opened his eyes and rose up on one arm. He stared at the young Gaffer for a long time before speaking. 'Your face is mine when I was a boy.'

'And mine will be yours when I am a man.'

The man sat up beside him and wrapped a blanket about them both.

'You need me,' Gaffer said.

'I'm uneasy, it's true.'

'I can tell you nothing you don't already know.'

His father bent forward, his hands to his head, the palms rubbing his temples. 'I want to know the things a son does with his father,' he said in anger.

Gaffer peered into his smouldering eyes. 'You will always be with me.'

'Never let them take what you should never give. Doubletalk would have you by the neck if they thought it would swell their pockets.'

The boy chuckled. 'It's true what they say. I'm as feisty as you!'

They shared a good laugh, and his father embraced him with such dire love.

'Pitch into them at every turn!' Gaffer exclaimed, with exuberance he had not felt in a long time.

'They'll not make a lackey out of you, my son.'

Their smiles erupted once again. Their hands tightly into one.

The boy stood up. His father eased back to the pillow and the boy covered him with the blankets. He watched his eyes close.

'It's Valentine's Day,' the man breathed as he fell back to sleep. 'Kiss her once for me.'

Gaffer's eyes filled with tears.

He left the room. Retraced his steps.

If anyone saw him, he railed, let them think it some spectre, some nightrunner come to warn them of what the day would bring.

On deck the early-morning light revealed the full measure of the scurrilous beast. Gaffer was tempted to invade the drill floor and have at the bosses, but he knew it was not them who called the tune. The ones that did were safe enough onshore.

He climbed stairs to the helicopter deck and stood in the middle of the bare expanse. He felt the brunt of the wind, heard its whistle through the criss-cross of the derrick. From a forward corner of the deck he set eyes on a lifeboat in its cradle. Held out by iron arms above the sea, as if the sea were its gentle mother ready to embrace it.

Gaffer circled the deck until, on its starboard edge, he reached a spot where there was nothing between him and the sea eighty feet below. He stood straight and stiff, a statue about to topple. He bellowed, a vehement outrage rising above the clamour of the drill site, a final, growling burst of contempt.

He bent his knees and sprang as far out as he could. His yell hung in the wake of the dive, then trailed off, until consumed with the boy in the waves.

The anchor cable blurred past, and he did not look back.

He jackknifed away from the towering shadow, beastly paw clawing at his back. He took leave, and damned their fate, and knew only that their senseless loss would not be without its consequence.

The aqueous reaches proved no escape. He held in the murkiness, foraging for sustenance, finding tenuous comfort in the cold silence.

A roaring echo then, distant chain of thunder, quake rumbling from the ocean floor! He knew it the crush of steel and concrete, pillars buckling to their knees into the sediment, derrick cast across the bottom like so much scrap.

It drove him away, far from the place, the echo chasing him.

He searched for solace in time. In a lifetime, a full seventy years before, in the iceberg waters to the southeast.

He trailed the bergs, their size an amazement, forcing him to know the grace to be had when nature builds her floating towers. He circled one and then another, dove along its white scarp to its very tip. Curved under it and shot up the other side.

Broke the surface, for the sheer distraction of it, and floated half in the water and half in the night air. The sky was moonless, but dotted with millions of stars, a dome, an everlasting shield.

There came to mind a scrap of verse from one of the shed's old battered books.

Dare he dream of other realms,
where would meet his kin?
Where might be found the earthly realm
that so eluded him.

Yet the pinpoints in the night sky were not without their earthly imprint. He thought at first it mere reflection, the sea so calm, the air so still.

He submerged and surfaced at a closer point.

Man-made they were. Porthole lights of a gigantic vessel—bow beneath the water, stern flung in the air.

Propeller wings dripping saltwater.

And now the night rang with the tumult of all that was loose within the ship, and now pitched higher with the screams of those clinging to the rails.

The ship's lights vanished, in a second. Only the stars now. In a screech of twisting metal, the vessel tore apart between two funnels, and the jagged, gaping bow end slipped away.

The stern seemed to hesitate, supremely vertical, people clasped to it, others dangling, dropping to the water from the steel cliff, before all was lost and the final edge of ocean liner slid into the sea.

Gaffer waded near a pan of ice, not far from lifeboats, nor the icy wake of the sunken ship where there were bodies in their hundreds.

Nor far from those alive, and their flailing screams.

The lifeboats did not move to rescue them. Gaffer neared one and heard their civil words.

'They'll swamp us.'

'We'll be goners.'

'They must understand our predicament,' said another through her furs. 'They must know how badly we feel for them.'

More cries for help, more desperate than before.

The lifeboat fell silent.

Gaffer dove, and surfaced before its bow.

'You have room for a dozen and more!'

They cowered at the sight of him and made their excuses.

'You're not one of us.' A uniform raised his oar.

'Perhaps he is,' a meek voice came. 'And he's only one.'

'Were you steerage, then?' piped the fur.

'Look at his skin! It's not natural colour. Definitely not English. Not from America.'

'From where, then?' said the fur.

'One of the colonies, most likely.'

'On leave, most likely, from the army.'

Gaffer sprang up and took hold of the boat. He rocked it violently.

'Dear God!'

They raised every oar against him.

No choice but to throw himself back into the water.

'Had you showed yourself a decent man ...'

But Gaffer was gone, straight down into the depths.

Above him the screams of the working men fell silent.

The seas covered its wounds. And in years to come, with wreaths thrown from ships passing in the night.

2001

She bided her time for him. Bundled in the tall beach grasses. Grasses the near-colour of her hair. Ethereal blue eyes fixed through the shifting stalks.

Himself rose from the water, to shoulder height, from the barnacled backside of Shag Rocks. A grievous lunge of his flaccid limbs to make it to the beach. He sank into the sludge of sand and water and sat, head limp between his knees.

The corner of his eye caught the rustling shift of her clothes through the grass. No surprise when she spoke. None at the brush of her leg against his arm.

'Found what you were after?'

No answer from him.

'And now you make no sense of it?' She halted. Then launched again. 'There is none. You are no more certain than ever you were.'

Viperous tongue. He cursed it.

'Rage chiselled into this rock of a place,' she avouched. 'Yours—but another smack of the hammer, you can be sure of that. Drive yourself insane if you think on it.'

He couldn't bear to have her rant on, as if what she said was meant to cure some poison in his brain.

At her feet he spit the glutinous crud that lined his lungs. His back stiffened. Across his face was scrawled the full measure of his temper.

'So that's the way of it,' she said. 'You no less a surly lot.'

'You're a damn plague.'

She laughed at him.

Then tried to soothe his wrath with a hand to his shoulder. He snatched at her wrist to fling it away.

Her strength was more than he was ready for. Nor the warm doeskin of her arm.

He looked into her eyes. They thrust past his ire and struck at the pith of him, man now, solitary to shore. He would have forced himself to damn her again had she not spoken first.

'Gaffer. A place to rest,' she said. 'I will take you to a place.'

'You. Shrew!'

She laughed.

'Bedraggled stray. Gypsy!'

'I know this land. For a thousand years.'

He mocked her audacity.

She took his hand. The touch of her like no other.

And as if given to a sweep of tide far up on land, he followed her. Silken stave of a girl unbuckling him, setting him in pursuit of her.

She led him past the houses, deserted now. Bare houses, bare yards, without the piles of firewood or corner garden plots. Not as much as a dog bark to tame the silence.

They passed the end of town, to a windswept clearing not far from another inlet of the sea. Over lichen and scrub patched with the last of the snow. To the mound of sod hut that undulated upon the land, like a heap of turf across a burial ground. A dwelling of sodden winter-kill, ash grey, matted, awaiting a spring.

They bent down and entered through a frame of logs. Inside she bared the red nuggets of the ember pit. Eased him to the hearth. Had him soak the warmth of it—heat to flesh that for so long had no need of it, that took to it now, water dog basking before the sun.

The girl took secret delight in his mutterings, even if the scattered pleasure-moans were against his will, even if there was nothing she could take for words of gratefulness.

Gaffer stretched his full length on the floor and fell into deep sleep.

Her humming gave way to a tuneful air, of an oaken ship, how its fearsome prow cut the horizon long ago. Of people blown back across the northern sea, not to set foot again upon this ground.

No mournful melody. Not her way to fix upon those that had forgotten her. But upon the raw, fitful creature before her now.

She smoothed salve along his limbs, her touch against the fibrous ridges of his muscle, thrilling at the curve of them. The secret of the lair of them, deep between his legs.

He awoke, days and nights past. His body no longer aching as it did, mended so the air into his lungs gave it cause to flex again and sit up stiff, in mortal fashion.

She had hot brew for him. Steam rose about his face. He drained the concoction down his gullet. He waved for more before the bowl had touched the ground, wiping the hand across his lips and casting an eye on her.

'I have you to thank.'

She nodded, his grudging gratitude a cause for more amusement than she would show.

And waited again for him to speak, to let him think he took the manly lead.

'One of us, you are?'

'Us? Would I have kept a vigil for you if I were not?'

It was no satisfaction to him. 'Here of your own choice?' he said.

'You ask such a thing, when all the others have scattered to the mainland?'

'Had they a choice?' he flared.

Pushed himself to his feet. Then, teeth like rocks grinding together, to his full height.

He stumbled once, but with sweeping stride fled the hut.

'Have sense, man. Why do you think I follow you?' she called after him, her anger as emphatic as his own. 'This place is as much of me as it is you!'

Not a falter in his gait.

'Drown in your own temper, will you!' she yelled.

He twisted sideways, turned his head back. 'How do I know you are not one of them? Luring us to think they have the answers. That we have no mind of our own!'

'You are talking rot!' She would say no more. She

watched as he strode away. His shoulders rigid, his arms two rigid oars.

He struck out toward his house.

Not one sign of life, but for the front porch where now the Alzheimer's wife replaced the man. She smiled to see someone, even if he was passing by.

'Skipper's gone,' she said, to the click of her knitting needles.

Stopped Gaffer in his tracks. He opened the gate and walked up to her. 'Not many like him. He had the stories.'

'Didn't remember a darn thing,' she said. 'Didn't know but he'd never been born in this place.'

Gaffer shook his head. 'He knew, all right. Put him in a fishing boat and he knew it.'

'Remembered you well enough, Gaffer. I'll say that much.'

She smiled at him. Hadn't missed a stitch. Gaffer walked slowly back down the path.

'Sorry to hear about your grandmother, Gaffer. I'd say she's chief cook and bottle washer at the Lord's table now.'

Sunk in him like a blade. He flew off, straight to his house.

Blinds and curtains closed. A van packed with furniture and boxes, idling in the driveway.

Found his mother in a bare kitchen. She wore a leather jacket and gold hoops of earrings. She broke then into tears. Out of sorts with the coat, with her make-up.

'Sweetheart,' she crooned. 'Dear, loving son.'

He stood a head taller than his mother now. She seemed not to care.

'Dear, sweet, loving Gaffer.'

'And Nan?'

'Didn't last long once it set in.' More tears. 'She talked about you all the time. Right to the very end.'

They held to each other, though it was strange—the perfume, the stiffened hair, the way her fingernails scraped the back of his neck.

'Gaffer, there's someone for you to meet.'

An outstretched hand and a smile as broad as a farmyard sky. 'How's it goin', dude? Call me Chuck.'

'We're heading out,' said his mother.

'I got connections in the record business, son. They're always scouting for a fresh look. Something different. And lordy, this place is different. Came up here to go huntin' big game, and done bagged me the next singing sensation. Seafaring-country we're going to call it. Your mother's going to be big time. Proper *thang,* what son, proper *thang.*'

Gaffer's guts churned at the sight of him. Seethed at the thought of his mother wooed by the hillbilly buck.

'What say, son, want to come along? Try your luck in the good ol' —'

'Not me. *Chuck.*'

'The fella knows his mind. Say that much for him, hon. Like a man who lays it out straight.'

His mother led Gaffer to another room, before his temper blew the stetsoned boor out of the kitchen.

She sat with him on a sofa. Put an arm around his shoulders. 'No gigs around here any more, Gaff. You know that. If I got to hit the road, might as well go all the way. What have I got to lose?'

Gaffer couldn't find it in him to tell her what was ripping his heart. She knew it already, of course. What more from him would make sense?

'The house is yours, Gaff. Make of it what you will. Don't think it could ever be the same.'

She embraced him. He held her, for the moment, and when the moment passed she stared at him, overcome by memories, as if there were doubts rising.

'Leave, if you have to. It'll not be me holding you back.'

'There's something better than this. I can't be living in a ghost town. You, Gaffer, you'll be gone again.'

He kissed her cheek. 'That's to remember him. Remember me.' Gaffer jerked his head toward the kitchen. 'And never let that infernal mouth make you forget where you came from.'

She stood up and straightened her clothes. Turned a nervous smile on Gaffer as her hands flitted about her hair. And left then with the grinning buckwheat Chuck.

'Now, dude, you be thinkin' about joinin' us, ya hear,' he said to Gaffer with them aboard the van.

He drove off, down the road. 'Graceland, here we come, hon,' he hollered.

Gaffer stood in the driveway and waved to his mother. *'Where the stars shine out their wonder,'* he sang. His voice fell off. *'And the seas roll up their thunder.'*

He strode back into the house. Sat in an armchair and back came all the voices that had ever filled the room. They spilled into the hallway and up the stairs, dozens of voices, generations of voices—the home women, the fish plant girls, the fishermen, their woodmen friends, the youngsters and teenage girls, and young men in their wool sock feet padding across the floor before dawn, about to set out with their fathers on the saltwater to haul the cod traps.

A fine ruckus of births and weddings and wakes, of scraping to keep food on the table, of the kitchen table end to end with Nan's breads and tarts and longevity loaves. Homemade smells wafting through the house, swirling amongst the revellers who give way to the mourners and turn back again to the toilers of every day after day.

Nan's voice he heard above them all. 'You're back, ya dear. Not cold in the ground I'm not and ya mother's outa here like a blue-ass fly. She's welcome to it, I'd say. That conniving puffpig—wouldn't eat me pork buns. Sure what is he atall? He's not one of us, not with a lip like that. He'd talk the cover off an iron pot.'

Gaffer rejoiced at her cannon fire rumbling through the house. He tramped from room to room, restaking claim to every one. The dwelling seized the thunder of his steps, and cheered him on.

He fell exhausted back to the living-room chair. He slumped there, cocooned in its cavalcade of stories, lulled by the murmur of their secrets, lost in the rumination of that past.

He woke to find the girl at the kitchen table.

A table spread with saltbeef and cabbage, turnip and carrot, potatoes, pease pudding and greens. Mugs of pot liquor. Warm bread bursting its pan. The open oven door announcing partridgeberry pie.

'It was here when I came,' she said.

Gaffer knew no reason to doubt it. 'Nan. Couldn't leave me without one last feed.'

He took to it as if it were sea air for his breathing. As he took to a sunrise vista of his Island.

Only after he had finished did he pay any attention to her. 'And what is it now?' he said.

'You must come with me.'

'Must,' he grunted.

He followed her, not because he had to. At a distance that asserted he did not care to be doing it, that she had some other motive in the scheming brain of hers.

The route took them up a moss-covered rock path, past twisted, stunted, half-dead spruce that had clung to the scant soil since the ice age, and would do so until the next one. He stopped from time to time, heedless of her, to scrounge handfuls of berries and stuff them in his mouth.

She laughed at the blue-stained mouth on him. Once, he emerged after a leak behind a bush, and she stopped. Waited for him to catch up. He drove her on with an impatient sweep of his hand.

They made it to the summit. 'Here,' she said. 'Suck in that air. For God's sake get it down into the pit of those lungs.'

Spread before them—an almighty sweep of the ocean.

'Glorious,' she intoned.

'Damned unpredictable,' he growled.

'That's why you take to it so easily.' Grinned at him.

He glared in her direction. To stifle that tongue.

She would have none of it. 'What's to make me think otherwise?'

'What bloody difference to you?'

'The weight of this rock on your shoulders!' she hissed. 'Must be hell. And to be so damned contrary at every stroke.'

'No one asked your kind.'

'*Your kind* is it now! So you are the sole heirs, the rightful ones. The only ones that belong to this place. Don't talk such shit!'

'We're the ones who built what is here. Slaved out a living. Buried our people beneath this rock.'

'Claim it, then. And what of us? And the red ochre tribes who came before us? And the ones who came before them?'

'They passed away.'

'Perhaps that is your fate as well. Pass off, make way for the next lot—'

He lunged, outstretched hand ready to seize her foul mouth. His head bursting at the gall of her.

She jumped aside and he stumbled to the ground.

He slowly rose again. His right hand turned into a fist.

She grabbed the fist, and with a twist of her body flung him to the ground, flat on his back. She fell atop him, knee pressed against his rib cage. Her anger equal to his own.

'When your tongue cannot do the job, you turn to savagery. You do nothing to deserve this place?'

'Off me!'

Her knee dug harder against his chest. 'Think I have learned nothing these thousand years? Think again, Gaffer.'

He grunted.

She slowly eased the pressure off his chest.

Stood up. Stared down at him. Took no pleasure in what she had done. Walked away with a few stiff words. 'Bloody noble as your fist, then you will never be satisfied.'

She sat on a rock and looked out to sea, keeping Gaffer in the corner of her eye.

He dragged himself to another rock, hand still clenched.

'Rid yourself of that fury. It does neither of us any good,' she said.

'Vixen. Minx. Wench!'

'My people called me Gudrin.'

His upper lip twisted with indifference.

'Suit yourself. You are not the first man I have flattened, if that is any consolation.'

'Get away from this place. You are not wanted. Hear me!'

She gazed down the shoreline, projecting her fair-skinned, bone-tight features. She spoke as if he had not uttered a word. 'It is for you to safeguard. True enough,' she said quietly. 'Not to hoard.'

She came suddenly to her feet. She had spied a broad pan of ice near the shore. A pack of men around a seal.

They smashed it with a gaff. Gloried in its torment. Poked it, kicked it, drew a knife to its quavering flesh.

'Savages!' she screeched at them. 'As if that creature roved these waters for you to do with as you wish!'

'Deny them supper, would you, woman!'

'They deserve none.'

'Ice hunting is our heritage.'

'Would you bloody your hands in sport, man!' She flung her arm in the direction of the ice. 'If that be your heritage then you are no better.'

He looked for cunning in her speech.

Looked at her savages, saw Skidder and his lackeys, the grinning fools. All for a video camera. He could not push himself enough to thrust her words back in her face.

What of his great-grandfather's days, what of the spring hunts, in vessels rancid with the blubber of seal carcasses, men sent scouring the ice floes, half fed, half frozen, to load the decks with tens of thousands of pelts, all for a pauper's wage? What of that? Not he who would deny his ancestors' bloodied sweat and toil.

'Not you,' she said.

'Who, then?' he snapped. 'Who, then! I am part of what has come before.' He swept his hand to the ice as she had done. 'And of this?'

She did not answer.

'Am I not?'

She shrugged. 'The female lot stayed ashore. Remember. To rear the young and tend the gardens and clean the house. Make the sealer a home,' she said, not without the edge of a cynic.

She left him to stand by himself at the edge of the cliff, staring at the blood-circus on the ice below. Cutthroats. Sleeveens. Desecrate the place would they and laugh at it like thugs?

This, his Island to defend? This loathsome spectacle for all the world.

He stood on the outermost edge of cliff, arms spread as if he were to fly. 'Kak-kak-KAK.' Hawk above its prey.

The blood-sport crew looked skyward. They cringed at the sight of him against the swirling clouds. A hand opened, knife dropped into the water, sank toward the bottom, a red haze scumming the surface.

Gaffer threw himself off the cliff. The girl ran to see his fall. He spiralled down, his bird cry rasping all the way.

'Kak. Kak. KAK!'

1977

Gaffer's dive thrust him through the scum of blood, drove a spray of it to kingdom come. Plummeted him straight down. His hand snagged the sinking knife.

Twisted, and turned past himself, back up the water channel to the surface, barely breaking it at the lip of an ice floe.

His hair frosted stiff to his skull. Bare-faced, unnoticed, he sank his eyes in what crowded the ice stage before him.

Another spectacle. Full-blown camera crew this time. Black cables snaking the ice, microphone boom, and doom of a gaggle of directors, PR princes, ogle-eyed young media brawn. Freezing their asses off.

All intent on the icy purr of BB. Brigitte. Bardot.

'Now, BB. For the camera, BB.'

The fluff *française,* lying on ice, ski-suited cat-woman of St.-Tropez, cooed into the eye of the camera. 'Don't let them butcher my bébé.'

The camera panned to her bébé and her arm snugly around the pup. The lens drew back to frame the duo. The pup whimpered on cue, its wet-black eyes looking *incroyable.*

'I want to kiss you,' BB whimpered to her bébé. 'I want to hold you to my bosom. Don't let them butcher BB's bébé, my cuddly white-coat bébé.'

At the kiss the bébé's mother, a portly hood-seal bitch left bereft of its offspring, rose up some distance across the ice, ready to rip apart anyone who would dare take away her suckling pup.

Only Gaffer caught sight of her.

He sank below the surface, emerged at a ledge on the other side of the floe, away from the commotion of BB and her boys. Knife for an ice pick, he hauled himself clear of the water. Flat to his belly, he slid forward, weapon at the ready.

The seal had swollen to the full height of her outrage. She struck out across the ice, ferocious waddle of fur. Teeth and forelimb claws primed for the onslaught.

Without warning there erupted the snorting bellow of the mother hood, on direct course for BB.

BB struck a new pose. Of terror at the ferocity of nature in the raw.

'BB!'

They were powerless to save her.

Only Gaffer, ice hunter, would fend off the attack. Knife poised above his head, he pursued the savage seal, chasing it down just as it was about to fling itself on the hapless BB.

He sank the knife through its fur.

BB cried out in pure ecstasy. The cameras rolled again, capturing her every euphoric syllable.

The knife-wheeling blur leapt over her, into the water, dragging the hood with him. The entourage gawked at each other as if they had gone snow-blind.

They shook it off. 'BB, you were delicious,' they crooned. 'And absolutely *incroyable.*'

Gaffer plunged free and clear and into unpolluted depths. He rejoiced at the ocean's broad expanse, at its endless, uncharted alleyways where a beast was no more than a beast.

The water nourished the hardy, encouraged their freedom. It shared its abundance, played no favourites. The peculiar, like Gaffer, were taken for no weaker or more cunning. Gaffer found shelter at the bottom and embraced its solitude.

The din of humankind was far away. The grievances that trod ice and earth seemed a distant dirge, without echo in his domain. He treasured the silence, the sameness, the sluggishness of change.

He settled in the sediment and took in the seaworld that encircled him. Many were the species unknown to him, as he to them; many flitted by and paid no heed.

Then the cod, fellow bottom dwellers, took notice of him there. Their tails stirred the bottom to expose him, as if to lay bare his intentions. They sensed his oddity. And his scanning of their numbers.

A dense school of them surrounded him, fish-eyed him, opened and shut their mouths in relentless curiosity.

'What's your game?' king-cod mouthed.

Gaffer showed no surprise. The lot had every right to know.

'An honourable one,' returned Gaffer.

'What, then?'

'To fight for you.'

Their fins quavered with amusement. 'No one gives a seal's dick about us, you witless bayman!'

'Boundless sea, remember, bayman. Hook and jig, and trawl and trap. Cast yer nets. Haul and cast again.'

'Only for us, half that crowd would be back in their old country digging fuckin' potatoes. That would give 'em something to sing about, all right.'

'Fish are in good numbers here and now,' Gaffer put to them.

'Good numbers, bayman! You need a hook in the gob to teach you a lesson.'

'Know something we don't?'

Gaffer couldn't bring himself to add any more.

'You want to talk fish, bayman, you should have seen us in our prime.'

'Ocean enough for everyone in those times.'

'Got no respect now.'

'Ah, never did. Just more of 'em, that's all.'

'Headed for disaster, what, bayman?'

Still Gaffer said nothing.

The cod milled about, in wait.

'Better get their heads screwed on right, or they're gonna pay for it.'

'They could use some fish-sense, that crowd.'

Gaffer agreed.

'Gluttonous fools!'

It was a sad lot that swam off and left Gaffer to his own bit of the ocean floor.

They shunned him now, as if he were the lowliest of its creatures, the dregs of their habitat.

Gaffer wriggled into the sediment. Hid himself as much as he could. He knew the sting of their distance. The disdain in every one of their kind that bothered to come near, their quick flick away from him. Even the scavengers were suspicious of his ways.

He kept to himself, found satisfaction in the solitude, beauty in the silence. Perfected that same sneer of distrust. Armoured himself with it when time came to make his way to deeper water.

He knew at once he had struck back on more abundant times. Cod in numbers he had only imagined. Majestic, impenetrable schools surging before him.

He headed for the surface. At the edge of a vast ice pack, a seal dove down. Made off with a meal of them.

Then bound out of the water ahead of him, onto the ice, wriggling its way back to the herd, back to its pup. Herd that peppered the ice for half a mile, mounds of fur indifferent to the North Atlantic bluster.

Beyond the far edge of the ice pack loomed a bloodhound ship, its ice-men swarming over the side, seven-foot length of gaff in hand. Agile cats, they dodged their way from pan to pan until they struck the solid ice.

Into the thick of it then, they were, the gaff their killing tool. The ice rang wild with a piteous chorus of suckling pups, their mothers scrambling into the water. Gave way to the cries of men glorying in the kill, and the rasp of blades across sharpening steel.

The ice splotched crimson with the gush of blood. Soaked the mitt-handed men who craved the pelt and thick of fat. It smeared their ragged clothes, dried atop the blood-crust from the day before.

They lashed pelts together and made their blood-trail to the ship. To the charm of the Cap'n at the rail.

'That's it, me lads. Leave 'em for the winch, and back at it agin!'

The lads were the devil's own boys for the kill. Gaffer saw the thirst in their eyes. Left him wanting to know what craved in their hearts.

At one he looked especially hard. Seen a picture of the man, he had, on his grandmother's bedroom wall. And the gaff in his hand—that from his uncle's shed, the very one.

His kin, he was! A devil of a sealer, he was.

The fellow slit the pup from throat to scuppers with one clean flick of his knife. He sculped the pup and lashed tow rope to the blubbered hide. Off he went.

Gaffer kept a keener's eye on him, followed him to the ship and back again across the ice. In fine spirits, he was, joker amongst the lot. Lively crowd altogether, traipsing off to find another patch of young ones.

Steady line of work-dirt sealing men weaving their way against the glare. Icelarks on the jaunt. Single-file, frosters on their skinboots clawing a route over the ice miles heaved and clumped together. His kin at the head of them, tow rope coiled across his chest, gaff in one hand, ship's flag in the other. Wool cap hauled over his ears to break the wind.

Gaffer followed at the floe's lip, sometimes under it, surfacing to keep steady sight of them. Finally they struck the patch, the bumper thick o' fat, they said. The fellow dug the flag staff into the ice.

'Now then, lads, Cap'n won't be satisfied till she's greased to the rails. Go to it, lads.'

Another blessed rally on the floes. A torrent of swile blood, and a steady haul of seal pelts to the marker flag. Piled them high they did, great mound of pelt and blubber, and yet they knew the Cap'n would be wanting more. Still the merchant ship-men did not have their fill.

Gaffer saw it coming—the thickening of the air with snow. At first the men paid no mind. Worked away, steady at it still, even with the steady rise of wind.

Turned into a bloody gale. The bloodhound ship nowhere to be seen. The men caught out on the ice, not able to make it back. He'd heard the tale too many times before.

He followed them, swam alongside the floe when they veered off course in the blinding storm. Such a rage of men. So far from the ship when darkness fell. He watched them huddle together, their clothes no match for the brunt of wind across the Arctic ice.

Gaffer languished in the water, their grief his own.

In the dead of night, upon this ice-scape, the moon revealed the hulking statues of men stiffened with the cold. Their arms clasped round each other, a friend's holding up a friend, arms of a father tight around his son. When the cold had done its worst, some toppled, ice-coated bronze of a people hardly to be remembered.

Gaffer sought his kin. Knew it was him struggling from man to man, urgent to hold the whisper of spirit in every one of them. Gaffer saw his own eyes in that hoarfrost face. Witness to his blighted hopes.

The man wandered aside, crumpled to his knees, searching for his own assurance he would outlast the storm. His eyes succumbed, fell shut, but stubbornly opened for another time.

'You'll not give in,' Gaffer yelled against the wind. 'You're not one to be hoisted on deck a frozen corpse.'

The fellow peered into the night, through the snow squall, past the edge of ice. Staggered to his feet again.

'That you, Cap'n?' his voice a murmur through the storm. 'We done our best.'

Gaffer would not abide his civil tongue. 'Done better than your best!'

It startled the fellow into drawing nearer. He halted at the very edge of the ice. Squinted.

'What breed of man?'

'Same as you.'

'Come to save us! Bless you. Bless you ...' The wind blew his words away.

'I cannot. It is yourselves who must rise up,' Gaffer shouted. 'Why let them make a drudge of you?'

His kin slumped to the ice. 'Who of our Island would dare defy the Cap'n? And have our families want for food? I fought to get this sealing berth ...'

He could protest no more. He fell across the ice.

Gaffer rose out of the water and touched the frost-bitten hand still holding to its gaff.

He slipped away then. The dawn was breaking. The storm had done its worst. And in the distance could be heard a faint whistle from the ship.

The man struggled to his feet and lamely went to gather the others who were left. To lead them in a line to the waiting ship.

Gaffer left the dead and their dying breed of men. The bloodied pans of ice. The swirl of television rites.

To make something of it all would take a labour

he could not bear. He retreated to the mindless depths. Drifted, dwelt on nothing but his own survival. Showed not much concern for even that.

Eventually he floated up from it and struck out for home. He cared not to think of what he passed. Sagas of the Island's sealing ways soaked with remorse and endless warring cries. Did no justice to a people scraping out a life on these far-flung shores.

Drew nearer them. Slowed his pace. There was not the urge to get to land as drove him there before.

He surfaced, but hung in the water, looking up and down the coast. Its inlets and bays abandoned now. Dulled with the wind and years that passed. What of this place? What of it still?

His cry a raw and mournful note. Desolate. Abandoned hope.

2009

He hauled himself ashore. She was there, as he suspected. With eyes no older. Not that he did more than glance at them.

Past her. He would not have her pawing him again.

Gudrin followed him. Sat near him on a barkless, weather-bleached log. She waited for him to speak.

He glanced at her again. She looked no wiser, if less eager with her tongue. She was smiling.

Back to him that smile of hers had come many times since last he laid eyes on her. As if he were some beast too dumb to know the difference? Did she not have the sense to see he would not be taken in?

'Who is left?' he said.

'A scattered few. The ones too sick. Or too contrary.'

'And you.' Said with some bark and spite.

She smiled again. 'Would you have it otherwise?'

'Here,' he grumbled. 'Show me what has changed.' He stood up at once and headed off.

'Not you,' she muttered. Louder then, 'I'm to follow? At your beck and call.' The cynic's voice, softened with an earthy drone.

He swung around. She had not moved.

'If you would.' He could be as caustic. 'You do consider yourself an inhabitant of this place?'

She would not favour him with an answer. But strode past him and took the lead.

Gaffer grunted, scored it with a curse word.

She ignored it. Led him through the place. Past the houses boarded up. The stores—signs faded, broken, pock-marked by shotgun shells. Bus shelter toppled to the ground. No place to wait, not that a bus would ever come.

The woman gone the way of the Alzheimer's man. Their house gone, too. Only a charred scar of it across their land. 'Broke in, they did, set fire to the place. Police hardly bother to come here any more.'

Gaffer stood at the broken gate. He had not known either of them beyond a few passing words. Had known their ways, though. Lichens to this rock.

'Who?'

'Need it be asked?' She turned her eyes toward the rumble in the distance.

Up the road they came, Skidder and his toadies, shaven-headed beerguts marching in their black clap boots. Gaffhooks for weapons in their fists. Their dirty hides fishscaled with tattoos.

They halted in front of the pair. Looked them up and down. Spit their contempt into the gravel at their feet. Spit rolled into dirtballs.

'What do you say for yourself, Gaffie boy?'

Nothing the idiot Skidder deserved to hear.

'Cod tongue-tied?' He roared in laughter with his kickass crew. 'Right, b'ys!'

Gaffer took the girl by the arm. About to get past them, loathsome scum.

'Swim off, will you?' He stepped in front of them. 'My fishface friend.' Chuckling.

He tilted his gaffhook, its point aimed between Gaffer's legs.

'Wouldn't want any damaged gear ...' His hyena mob let loose. 'Eh?'

It jerked them into a frenzy of muscled insults. Rabid, leathered rats restless at the promise of a kill.

Gaffer dared not move. But glared at them, hatred growling in his brains.

Gudrin, steel spring for her leg, kicked the gaffhook to hell. Stunned the swine. She grabbed Gaffer by the arm and dragged him on. Skidder and his scum tore after them.

She swung around and struck her foot into a gut, crumbled the prick into the ditch. Ground the others to a stop.

The pair went on, did not look back. Left them to lick their wounds and flail the air with snarling notice of revenge.

Gaffer hurried the girl to his house. Shut themselves inside, shut out the godawful noise. Only then did he say what he knew had to be said.

'You surprise me again. I am in your debt.'

She was amused by his reticence still. And did not attempt to hide it.

'Of course, what else is there for you to do,' he said, 'but ready yourself for such a thing.'

'Sorry I could not spare your pride!'

'It remains intact.' He pushed a grin at her.

She made for him, grabbed him by the shoulders. He tried to defend himself, but attacking him was not her intent.

She kissed him roughly on the lips. And drew away from him just as quickly. Left him with a look on his face no worse than if he'd been whacked in the back of his head.

'You needed that,' she said. Though not without some embarrassment herself. She started to make them something hot to drink.

Soup. Like his mother would make when he was a boy, when first he had taken to the water.

Gaffer sat at the kitchen table, unable to speak. She stood at the stove, her back to him, adding ingredients to the soup, stirring it all the while.

He found letters from his mother on the table, a small package. The letters told of her nightclub act, her demo tape, her and Buckboy's ride down the neon road of semi-sweet success. Gaffer opened the package and played the tape.

He hardly recognized her voice. Southern now. Bucky's tough, sweet, sexy Southern belle. He shut it off.

He took a hot bath, it ringing in his ears.

He let his whole self sink below the surface, to cleanse himself of all the crud this place had left for him. Still, when his head rose up again, her damn twang was there, and would not disappear, dirt in an open wound.

At the kitchen table Gudrin served him the soup. It brought back to him fine and decent memories of his mother. Brought back how often she had told him she belonged in this house.

He hardly looked at the girl. Though he knew

she kept her eyes on him. She ladled him more of the soup and said nothing. Let his head dwell somewhere else.

Restless, he was. When he was done with the meal he searched the house for something, knew not what, that needed to be found. He rummaged from room to room, through drawers and attic trunks, and ancient metal boxes under the beds. What finally he found was the likeness of the ice-hunter, the young sealer man he had seen upon the floes.

He stood stiffly, with wife and child, before this very house. The fellow who went to the floes every year for twenty more. Died no poorer. No richer either. Died before his TB wife and eleven of his dozen kids. Died happy, they said, 'cause he had his fish dried and his potatoes dug, ready for the winter.

Gaffer unearthed older pictures still. A grizzled, ancient crowd of brothers, and the long-skirted, grim-faced row of seated wives. Stories had it they got along no better than it looked, though they fished from the same boat, and worked their plots of land side by side, and raised a strapping brood of youngsters.

Youngsters who stuck to this place, never budged except for the two who got blown to hell along the Somme. Women who married men from the place. Men who married women from up the shore. Carried their women pregnant across thresholds of houses built next to their parents' own.

There were pictures of the land, its cabbage growers and berry pickers. Mostly the pictures were of the sea. Skiffs and schooners, men and their boats geared up for the fish. Flakes of split and salted cod to cure before the sun, endless stretches of the stuff. The reason for sailing across that sea, the reason for holding to that land.

Gudrin came and sat by him. Told him of the times when she had seen such things. When the place was swarming with young maidens and women. The men and lads sailing off aboard their boats. Fair marvellous sight it was, she said, as if what she was speaking of were yesterday.

'Who *are* you, then?' His manner blunt, more civil though than any he had used with her before.

'Same as you. Not one to see this Island founder.'

She had been there to meet him each time he came ashore. And would be there again. No way to be free of her. Not that he wished it any more.

When she left the house, he went to a kitchen window and followed her until she disappeared through the trees behind the house. He would not rid his head of her, the conviction of her stride, the tautness of her figure, her brush of yellow hair.

Gaffer stayed alone in the house. Not a breath but his own, not a sound but the sound of his wandering between the rooms, the shift of his naked feet across the dusty wooden floors. It was more than he could abide.

He took the place and made it his own. Cleaned it and fixed it, inside and out. Shouldered home abandoned logs. Sawed them and split them, set some afire in the stove.

Dug a square of ground. Tilled the soil, added seaweed for the fertilizer. Sowed his vegetables in perfect rows. Watered them faithfully. Watched the garden sprout, the earth raise up the shoots, glorying in what it could offer anyone who took the time.

He inhaled the sweet pleasures of it all, at what he brought to fallow ground.

And in the evenings, after the work was done, he walked the empty streets, watching for her.

He knew she would not show herself, that he would have to go in search of her. Show a need for her. Had he a one?

He grew wanting of someone there, his labour done, the evening echoing of more than him at rest. He read, and wrote the journal of his day, and took to looking at the heavens. Losing himself in the thought of an earth that was a fleck of dust, swirling in the dustbowl of the sky.

One evening he took a forest path that brought him to a church. The place of pride in his grandmother's heart.

Gaffer looked about it curiously, it cold and vacant now. Altar bare. Stained-glass window the only life about the place. In wonder at the reverence that hung within it still, his gaze ran slowly from arch to arch, beam across hand-cut beam.

'A shell of what it always was.' A voice from a

dark choir corner. 'From the time they cut the timbers, rose them up with block and tackle. My father's people built that very pew. Them, and our family after them, sat in it a hundred years and more.'

The fellow stood up, screwdriver and crowbar in his hands.

'The choir sings no more. And I'll take away that pew before the vandals have it their way.'

Gaffer worked with him to rescue it. Dislodged it from the floor. Heft it up and lugged it past the double doors. The fellow went off with the pew toppled into the box of his decrepit pickup truck.

The wind rose, whistled through the church, lament for the days when the bell drowned it out and the people came in droves. When the organ filled the rafters and parsons stirred the sinners to join the holy throngs.

Gaffer sat stiffly, with his demons, insisting on answers to it all. None dared enter there. He sank his length along the pew. Let the darkness fall down around him, cover him for the night. He fell into sombre sleep.

A thunderclap of breaking glass jerked him to his feet. Light of dawn flared in where the Sea of Galilee had washed before. A screech of tires and the ratpack was gone, their hideous laughter in their wake.

The village all came when they heard it. The fellow who had taken home his pew. The hangers-on, the stragglers, those set to die where they had been born. The scattered few. The contrary ones. Those too sick to know the difference.

'We'll have no more of this,' said one.

'We'll not see our faith mocked by hooligans, too stunned to hold to anything.'

And in a pact among themselves, the tribe of souls agreed they would set the place afire, let the timbers return to the place from whence they came. They emptied the church of the remnants of its sacred days. And in the spot where once had stood the font of their baptisms, they built a pyre. Broken fence palings, the keels of boats that were never built, sawdust from the mill that would not hum again.

That night they set fire to it. Stood back and

watched it blaze. Tongues of flames soared through its belfry, searched out the sky. Visible for miles around, with no one worthy of the view. It brought only the scavengers, revving their throaty engines just outside the place.

At dawn, when the others had left the smouldering pile, they skulked closer and hunched around the heat and drank their beer. Dogmen, they grew braver still. They drained their piss and heard it sizzle and laughed to see the steam rise and drift away.

Gaffer wandered from the sight of them staggering through their serpent dance. He rambled off in search of something to resemble the promise of his youth.

He waited hours within the sheltered cove that bore him capelin as a boy. No fish came to spawn. He dug in the sand and planted his feet and the sea came in and washed them naked once again. A lone gull circled like a seahawk overhead.

Finally, he sank into a tidal pool and huddled against its wall of rock. He found whore's eggs. Spiny urchins stuck tight to the rock. He crushed them open and sucked them out. A seal he was, a damn lone seal drove to shore.

He went in search of the girl. Did not dwell on why he wanted her. Enough that he gave up denying that he did.

He drew closer to her place, grew more fearful that harm had come to her. From the scrubby trees flicked ragged bits of fluorescent plastic tape. Her dwelling's path worn to black and barren peat. Incised with brutal tire treads.

Her door was solid shut. He pounded it with his fist.

She flung it open and stood there with a frightful blade above her head. Her eyes fierce as any he had known.

The blade fell by her side. 'You.' Word flung with a querulous laugh. 'Not through any of your doing am I safe. And not if I had given the scum the chance.'

Now anger stiffened him.

'Change of heart. How manly of you. Fishguts.'

He let her have her prod at him. But held at the

door and would not pull back a fraction of a step.

She had her way. Had him stand there and push out his excuse. She took in the strain at every word. Took satisfaction in much of it.

'Wasn't asking much,' she said. 'Damn more than you were willing to give.'

He did not move. Even when she turned her back and disappeared from sight.

'What now?' he called.

'It's you who must decide.'

Gaffer hawked and cleared his throat, faked a show of his uncertainty.

'A charmer! The way you foul my house like some wordless halfwit.'

'Enough.'

'Say it, then. I'll shut up.'

The most welcome notion yet he heard. Tempted, he was, to say so, but knew better of it.

'The two of us—a safeguard for each other.'

The weight of her silence pressed him on.

'I know myself needing you, in spite of all I might have said. Or have not done.'

'You find yourself to be a man after all.'

'And you behave like you have no use for me, when I know damn well you do!'

'Use? It is not use, man.' She showed herself, and the fervour in her stare. 'Look me in the eye and tell me you have no more than *use* for me. Tell me, and I'll call you a liar.'

'What is it I have for you? What is it but something to die away and leave me in torment about what should have been.'

'You fear it, then.'

'Fear it? What future is there for either of us? I want only for each of us to sustain the other.'

'And to hell with the reason for it!'

The flare of her words drove a spike between them. He stalked off, desperate to be out of her sight.

She called to him but once. 'Come back when you have found what *should have been.*'

He would not reply. But headed for the sea, knowing for damn sure he would find more than she would ever know.

1787

He did not have far to go.

Off the headland, the waters dense with cod. Impossible to manoeuvre through. He let himself be carried along, as if he were one of them. Some not far off his size.

Strong in their numbers, an accepting lot, but quick to have it known that what was done, was done their way.

'Act like one of us,' they said, 'and you'll take charge.'

'Of what?' Gaffer asked, perplexed.

They laughed. Peered at him as if to say what could they expect, to judge by his peculiar ways.

'Of this very Island whose rock sticks out like a smack in the cod's-head.'

'Dunce!' said another. 'Why do you think anyone ever comes to this godforsaken rock? Not for the good of their health. Dunce!'

'For fish, fool.'

'There's one of their damn sorry skiffs.'

Gaffer looked upward to see the sea-scabbed bottom of a boat.

'Pitiful. Hardly trust it enough to put an oar to its gunwale.'

'Got no choice, poor bugger.'

'Most years he gets hes nets around enough of us to keep him happy.'

'Keep hes merchant man happy, you mean.'

'Haven't got a bloody prayer of seeing much for all hes slave work. Merchant man pays him back in flour and molasses. Enough to keep he and hes family from starvin' off the face of the earth.'

'Fools for comin'. Fools for staying once they got

here. The ones with the sense gave up this place long ago and took off south.'

'Smart. Yes,' they all said, 'damn smart and they damn well know it, too.'

Gaffer grunted. 'Yankee turncoats.'

They laughed at him. 'You've not the sense to see it any other way.'

'Couldn't take it,' countered Gaffer. 'Takes a tough breed to survive the Island. It's the weak-willed what gives up. Don't want them here anyway.'

They called him a moron and drove him out of their lot. Chased him till he didn't know where he was going. Straight into the fisherman's net.

'Serves you right. A queer fish you are and you deserve no better than to be gutted and salted and dried for some English trollop to have for her dinner.' Their laughter rang through the water.

And up he was hauled out of the sea and over the gunwale amongst a miserable crowd of unfortunates.

And dumped onto the bottom of the boat. He slid with the avalanche of cod to the bow, out of sight of the fisherman still struggling with his nets.

Gaffer perched himself on the bow seat before the fisherman was done his work. He pressed his hair back from his face. Hauled the back of his hand across his mouth to smear away the cod slime. Spit off the rest of it.

The fellow lurched at the sight of him. Grabbed the gunwale to keep from buckling under the dread of him.

'Who you be?' he croaked, pale as his boot-leather face could ever get. 'A fetch? If me brains was soaked with rum, I might believe it, but not two drops have passed me lips 'tis months. I swear. Come to tow me off for me everlasting rest? I'd go willing except for leaving Sarah Jane and young Tom and the maidens.'

'No,' said Gaffer, though it did not ease the fellow's fear.

'What, then? I done nothing to deserve you, have I? I've worked me best. He's pleased with me catch and there's no one does a better job at dryin' fish along this coast. That's for fair and certain.'

'Come to give you a hand,' said Gaffer.

'Stowed away under me gear? Run away from up the shore? Not been treatin' you so well, is they?'

Gaffer nodded.

'Sure you looks like something hauled t'rough a knot hole. What have you got done to yerself?'

'I'm the finest kind.'

'Can you split and gut a fish? Did yer father teach you that much?'

Gaffer said nothing.

'Can't stay here unless you can earn yer keep,' he said, getting brave now. 'I'll ship you back with the next boat I sees goin' yer way.'

'That you won't. I'll do me share. There'll be no doubt about that.'

The fellow put oars in the water. Began the row back to shore, casting a steady eye on Gaffer all the while. He wasn't about to be taken for a fool, have a young devil come after him with the boat hook and make off with his skiff.

Gaffer put the fellow's mind to rest. He leaned forward, a prowhead, and set his eyes on shore.

They rounded the headland. The hills and lie of the land were what he knew, though the woods skirted the shoreline in places. And but one dwelling, it up from the shore on the first piece of level ground. Wharf, and shed, and fish flakes the most of it. There was a woman and youngsters bent over the flakes, spreading the fish to dry in the first sun of the day.

Gaffer caught sight of someone beyond them all, in the distance, pale hair racing from the bare rock into the woods.

'There!' He pointed. 'Who is it?'

The fellow squinted. 'Not for me to know.' He shook his head sternly. 'You neither. She be no trouble to us.'

Gaffer would not speak of her again.

'Sarah!' the fellow called when he was near enough to be heard. 'Look at what I got aboard the boat. Drowned rat from up the shore.' He had a laugh at that. Brave fellow now he was.

Sarah straightened up slowly, sweat-soaked in tattered skirts. She wiped her face with her sleeve and looked him over with a furrowed brow. She was not keen to be giving her approval so easily.

'Eager to work, he is.'

'That so,' she scoffed. 'He'll be a fool, then. We've nothing to pay him.'

'Not pay I want,' said Gaffer. 'Good company is all.'

Her suspicion deepened.

'He's a harmless lad,' the fellow said to her. 'Though what work he'll get out of those scrawny arms I fair have me doubts.'

Gaffer jumped up and onto the wharf in one quick motion, to prove he was more sound of life and limb than either of them would have it.

It did pittance to change her mind. She drew her face near his, led by its quizzical beak. 'You one of the merchant's men, come to spy? He'd have me out of here if he had half the chance. No use for women on this coast. You tell him I'll not be budging, me nor any of the maidens. This family be here to stay. And there'll be more joining us, you tell him that, next fishing season.'

'He not be a spy, I tells you, Sarah. He not be the governor's man, neither.'

'Show me what work you'll have me do,' said Gaffer, to bury the straggling bit of doubt.

The fellow stuck his gaff into one of the cod lying in the bottom of his boat and heaved the fish onto the wharf. 'Let's see how handy you be at the splittin' table. Hand him a knife, Sarah, we haves a look at what he got hesself into.' A raucous laugh.

Gaffer slapped the fish onto the splitting table. Took the knife to it. He slid the blade down the belly and flicked away the guts with a deftness that pleased the fisherman and quelled the fermenting notions of his wife. She said no more against him.

Young Tom and all three of his sisters gathered on the wharf to see what he was about. A new face in the Cove was a curious sight, all the more because he was young and bore with him no sign of a wife.

The eldest of the lot, Ella, could scarcely believe her good fortune. She'd not seen anyone of marrying age since her mother dragged her aboard the ship and away from the sweet lips of some gadabout in Weymouth town. She had bawled on deck half the time it took to cross the Atlantic, and when she was not heaving with seasickness, brooded in the ship's stinking hold the other half.

She set her eye on Gaffer. No matter that he was not the least bit keen on her. No matter that he wanted to be spending his time at her father's fish. She lurked in the background of their every discourse, her demure glances giving way to a never-ending smile.

'Ella,' her father would say, 'be off with you now. Gaffer will have hes time for you when the work is done.' To Gaffer he would add, 'She's a fine lass. Strong as an ox. Don't let that look fool you. She knows her place. Haven't see any young men about, 'tis all.'

Gaffer steered clear of her as much as he knew how, though it was no easy job. The only safe place was in the boat, out the Cove to the fishing grounds. There he found some peace of mind.

No trouble each morning to make a catch, though the boat was not a big one, and the gear had seen better days. The fellow could have sunk the boat with cod had he wanted to, but he kept a stern eye on her watermark and had a good head for the wind.

'You'd not want to be caught out here in a storm o' wind. You'd not last long. I've seen seamen, good ones, too, banged up on rocks, not a sign o' life left in 'em. Salted away then and carried back to England, not so much as a penny for their poor widows.'

'Hard life,' said Gaffer. 'This place—hardly fit, is it, for man or beast?' He hung in wait for the fellow's word.

He wasn't long to come back at him. 'I'll not say that. I left worse, for sure. At Candlemas, now, the wind driving snow and ice broadside in yer face, not a letup, and not a sign of spring for months to come, I thinks of the old country, I do. And longs for it. But that is quick forgot when the sun is rising up out of the water and all around is land that hardly a man has laid hes foot to before.'

It roused the pith of a young Gaffer to hear the fellow go on so, and see him look to shore and the hills beyond it with a strong heart for his country. The early-morning sun gave the sea a glimmer, a brilliant sheen that promised benevolent days to come, a life that could get better for he and Sarah and Tom and the maidens.

'—Tis true,' he said, 'we depends awful on the merchant man, we do. At the season's end he takes the catch and sets the price, and gives us back in food and gear, but we not be begrudging him, for 'tis he who set me in this place and he who keeps us body and soul together.'

Gaffer could see the red, raw hands and the blisters about his wrists, saltwater pups he called them. No life for a sluggard. What rewards he had were but a scrap to that of the rogue who sucked away his catch.

'Will you not have your fair share of this country? It's you and your kind what can make it grow and prosper.'

'Prosper?' the fellow said with a leery eye. 'Not for me to see. Not on this shore. Not in the days God got left for me on this earth.' He brought a hefty laugh upon himself.

Gaffer heard nothing in his words to warrant it. 'You'll not have me agreeing with you, then. A man

who does not see justice in his own life cannot expect
to prosper.'

The fellow laughed again.

'You listen good.' He looked Gaffer hard in the
eye. 'We keeps ourselves from going hungry. And
some years it gets better than the one before. We
keeps warm enough in winter to get through to the
spring, and, next year, please the Lord, there'll be
another family here in this cove. And then another
and another. But prosper? I'll not know what it is to
prosper.'

'Have you no ambition, man?' Gaffer could not
hold back his anger. 'Are you to remain in servitude
all your life?'

'What would you have me do?'

Gaffer would not be quarrelling with the fellow.
Stood side by side with him. Saltwater and net twine
working calluses into his own fisherman's hands. Until
their catch was had, the codfish lot, the merchant's
pride. They took to shore, their duty done.

Sarah had civil words for him. And eyed his every
move. Only when Gaffer saw her whisper to the

daughter, and how it gladdened the heart of the tittering Ella, did he realize her intentions.

Ella sidled up to him at the splitting table. She was no slacker with a knife, and could flick cod livers in the oil barrel with a sweet twist of her wrist. She smiled his way and slit the belly of another fish.

When the day's work was done, and Gaffer had shared their meal of fish and potatoes, he snuck away to the bald scrapes of hills that overlooked their dwelling place. Imagined it in winter days, smoke rising from the chimney, frost enough to drive every beast into their holes. Imagined days when it mattered nothing what they had to call their own. When one another was all that kept them fierce enough to survive.

He lay back among the moss and scruff of bushes clinging to the rocks. Thought on his people and how they came to root themselves upon the shore. Some sea-brawn wayfaring crowd that took hold and held like dogs. Not about to give in to the smack of weather or the devil's own claw of the merchant man.

They would survive. And never let go without the fight.

He was not long settled to his spot when the rustle of her skirts startled him awake. His eyes, squinted at the sun, Ella took for scorn, and suddenly flopped down in the bushes next to him.

'Am I no match for the fish-maids down the shore? Too ugly am I for you to even cast your eyes on me?' She mourned her fate, her bitter, wretched fate, as she would have it. 'I was not for coming to this godforsaken hole,' she whined. 'What is here but stinking fish. No men to know the woman that I am.' The last gave rise to a full-blown wail. Her flower wilted.

'Ella,' he said. No tender entreaty. A blunt call to give up her foolish ways and make of herself someone a man could take to. 'He will come along. Surely. He will see in you someone to hold hard and long to this place. You will give rise to a fine brood of youngsters to run about the Cove and make it your own.'

It stirred her heart. It rose up her bosom, swelled it with a yearning Gaffer did not foresee. She wiped her tears with her sleeve and looked upon him with eyes red with longing.

She gave him no time to get away. She was on him like a fertile cat, her mouth on his, her hand clutching his rump and twisting her pelvis against his own. Her ardour was not to be repelled.

The smell of fish guts had not left her clothes. Her twists and turns stirred it to disheartening heights.

He could embrace not a smidgen of the lust that had taken hold of her. Trapped, he was, in a circumstance that would have quashed a lesser man. He struggled, and in the end was able to pry a gap between them.

Suddenly, Ella's amorous advances fell limp. She heaved herself away from him and collapsed. The mound of her rose and fell, and began to quake with sobs.

'Ella,' he said, though with care not to sound any regret for having spurned her so.

'Get away,' she hissed. The wounded one.

'You're deserving of a better man than I.'

'Out of my sight, you.'

'You have no use for me, I know.'

'None,' she sobbed. 'You are no more use than a sculpin fish. And with a mouth on you as big. Get clear of me.'

'I meant no harm.'

'Gutless!'

Gaffer could see no course but to retreat from her. He shifted away, sorry to leave her sobbing so. And now she wailed, so loud it echoed through the Cove.

It brought the fisherman and his wife. They set sights on Gaffer, wrathful sights, after they espied the lump figure of their daughter in the grass.

'What have you done to our Ella?' the wife shrieked his way. 'You shameless cur! Unleashed your manhood on our dear girl? Run, will you, you devilskin! I'll make away with you with my own bare hands!'

The fisherman grabbed a boat hook and took after him. 'Two-faced blood-of-a-bitch!' he yelled. 'Get back from where you came. You'll not have your way with our girl.'

Gaffer raced off. Stumbled once he did, foot twisted in a bog hole. Dragged himself up again, face hauled through a snarl of alders and black spruce.

In his bleeding daze he brushed past the blur of yellow hair and a derisive smile. He wiped the blood from his eyes, but would not dare hold back to search her out.

He broke through to the grass ground on the bank, jumped and tumbled down its sand, the fisherman behind him still. Boat hook cutting the air, threatening to rip his arse.

Gaffer made it to the saltwater, plunged in, drove himself to the bottom, out of sight of all who saw nothing in him but a ruttish rogue. Gaffer surfaced near the headland, looked back at the fisherman barking still from the landwash. The boat hook a lance now. 'No better than the redskins, you're not!' he screamed. 'Steal the eyes outa your head, and come back for the holes.'

Gaffer sagged in the water. His heart sank.

He came again to life at the sound of Buckley's chaw and chatter.

'Gaff, you're not surprised?'

He saw the goat staring back at him from the grass of the headland.

'Hard to know what to think,' said Gaffer, and sagged again.

'Hard to think there's not more to know,' said Buckley, and chuckled at his wit. 'They're a tough breed. Have to be. Survive 'cause they're an iron stake into that rock. Not going to shift, unless the rock shifts with them.'

'That so?'

'Ella'll get her man, needn't you worry. And her brood of youngsters.' Buckley chuckled once again.

'Good for her.'

'And look what that give rise to. Cove filled up till what you had was as good and proper a place as ever there was on this Island.'

Gaffer looked none too contented still.

Buckley seemed to know what was on his mind. 'They weren't prime stock, 'tis true. Everyman thinks he's from the best of what came before. But hard workers they were, and full of gumption after a spell.

Broke away from that scoundrel of a merchant man. Built up a place for you and your kind.'

'For what hell good it did.'

'Gaffer!' Buckley's bark hit him square in the face. 'You're not about to give in to it? You're not about to let all what's come before pass off for nothing. No, by the dyin' reevin's, you're not!' Buckley flared his nostrils, snatched up a gobful of grass and chawed on it with iron jaws.

Gaffer looked into his wise old cantankerous eyes. And looked away, shamefaced. He swam off.

'Gaffer!' Buckley called. 'You do what you see fit. It's you what got to live, the best way you know how.'

Buckley's eyes followed him all the way out to sea. To where he jackknifed beneath the waves.

2027

He strode out of the water, set for Gudrin, face-to-face. Stood upright on the beach rocks. Swept his eyes in every direction. Nothing. Except a dirt-brown gull squawking at him, expecting food.

No Gudrin. No sign of her having been there.

Panicked him. Forced himself, limp and paining, to stride on a course for her place. Past what remained of the houses. Dead dwellings for rodents and thieves, what weren't charred timbers caved in on one another. Family detritus for the earth to gather into itself.

Gaffer's sprint triggered a distant roar. His head jerked. What had been the water tower, now a gawking glassed-in cage. Red flashing beacon atop it. A scramble of men down the zig-zag of stairs to the roar of engines on the ground.

Gaffer stumbled on, fast as his limbs were willing. His heart beating hell-time. Fear of what he would find, fear of what would find him.

'Gudrin!' he yelled, pitching his voice ahead of him. He sighted her place through the trees and the fog. A better view of it when he broke out to the open marsh. His voice lost now in the engine roar behind him.

He glanced over his shoulder. Troop of guards on ATVs, acid-yellow searchlights bobbing across the ridges of the marsh. At the lead, riding his rig stand-up, was Skidder. Oil-black uniform, silver trim spit-polished, wedge of dark glasses wrapped around his face. A deadly black beetle-faced grinning punk.

'Gaffer!' he yelled. 'Your ass is numbered, boy.'

His rig spit a thunderous crackle, its front tire reared into midair. It bolted ahead of the pack. Gaffer lunged forward, lone bedraggled wolf, hunted for extinction.

Gudrin saved him. Threw open her door. Threw up her barrier when he was safe within.

'Skidder!' she blared and flung a gaff through the air with an almighty thrust. It pierced the front tire, blew Skidder's ass into the air. He landed, a stump in his gut.

His toadies pitched to a stop behind him. They flexed a line of submachines, every barrel trained on her.

'Call them off, Skidder! Touch me and that boss of yours will grind your brains to gullshit.'

Skidder knew it, too. He struggled to his feet and waved them off. He peered at Gudrin through swelling eyes.

'If it was up to me, hag, I'd blow you off the face of the earth.'

Skidder barked an order to hitch chain to the vehicle and haul it away. He hobbled aboard another and was gone with a finger jabbing the air and loud hawking spit rifled to the ground.

Gudrin glared their way until they were out of sight.

Gaffer lay sprawled across the floor. She helped him to a stool. A stream of thankfulness from him, nothing she had heard from him before.

'What stopped them?' he said.

'They know who calls the shots, and it's not the likes of them.'

'Who?'

She helped him to his feet. Led him outside. She pointed to a chain-link fence, ten feet high, if not more, running to the edge of the cliff. In the other direction it disappeared through the spruce, though he could see distant glimpses of it on higher ground.

'The whole way around, past the Gulch,' she said. 'The whole Cove. Bought every bit of land that had title. Government gave them the rest.'

'Who?'

She shrugged. 'Some slime of a front man. Hired Skidder and his clowns to guard the place. Nothing gets touched. Including me. Thwarted Skidder's bloody scheme.'

Damned them all, Gaffer did, damned them right to hell. 'Not a *preserve,* this is not!'

'It is now.' She stared into his eyes. 'Fish plant's been gutted of its equipment long ago. Not a boat to haul in a fish. Not a fish to haul in if there was a boat. Everyone's gone to the mainland, Gaffer. And what were too old to go are dead. Every one of them.'

'Skidder and the boys didn't go. Too bloody stunned?' His voice flew higher. 'What does that say about us?'

'Says the time's come to face up to it. What's the use of perching on this rock like some damn gull?'

He swerved away, made for the fence at the edge of the cliff. Grabbed hold with both his hands. A jolt blew him to the ground, landed him on a rock looking down into the sea. There erupted the high cackle of a siren, as if it were a laugh directly from Skidder's gob.

Gudrin was at his side, but said nothing.

Their silence swirled with the sea to shore. It twisted in the curl of waves. Coiled, and pounded the rocks, roaring at such a sorry sight.

Still no words, even when she wrapped her arm around his shoulder. But neither did he shun her hold on him. Her affection settled in, needing him. He found comfort in the wilful strength of it.

After a time he fell back upon the grass. She held herself against his back, arm tight against his chest. Wind came up and rain swept across them, though they held to the spot. After the rain had passed, they rose up together, two sodden creatures of the marsh, and in her dwelling they dried themselves before the fire.

The time came that he had to go to his house, though he dreaded it. She went with him, and from time to time along the road, he passed to her a fearful look. She would not tell him what she knew, but held tightly to his hand.

He saw first the fence, the same unscalable chain link. Rectangled, a brutish height, threatening back anyone who went near. Sign lashed over the lock of its only entrance: Keep Out.

Through the fence he could see the house, every bit as he remembered it. Grass cut. Vegetables growing in the garden plot. Flowers—dahlias, peonies, grandmother's wild roses.

Gaffer heaved a boulder at the lock. It sizzled with electricity. A speaker monotone droned a warning to stand back or face the consequences. Gaffer bellowed in anger. Heaved an even bigger rock before it was done. 'Say it again and I'll pulverize that scum face of yours!'

The crackle of Skidder's laugh.

Gudrin held him back. Her words made it no easier. He dragged himself clear of it. Then in a tear made for his uncle's fishing shed.

She yelled after him.

He had to see for himself. See that it, too, was some preserve. Blocked from anyone going near. Chain link, though there was no enclosing it all. Not what hung above the saltwater. Gaffer dove into the water and swam around the back of it. Hauled himself up the piles and onto the wharf.

Burst into the shed soaking wet. A wild fright for the fellow sitting at a computer, fingers to the keyboard, surrounded by mounds of fishing gear.

'Who are you?' he demanded, jumping to his feet and grabbing a boat hook. 'You're not authorized.'

Gaffer glared at him. 'None of this is yours.'

'This is a heritage site. I am classifying the artifacts, bucko.'

Gaffer snarled at his talk and made for the cod jiggers and twine needles on the table.

'Stand clear!' the fellow yelled, brandishing the hook. 'I'll not have you contaminate the artifacts.'

'And I'll not have you make a fool of this place!'

'Snap out of it, you ingrate. We're in a new millennium. This is a new economy.'

Gaffer's fists tightened.

'We're not forgetting the past, my friend. We're preserving it. Everything in this shed will have a label. And every label will have a number inputted into this data bank with corresponding graphic. Plus, no doubt, some entrepreneur will bring out the coffee-table book. And there you will have it all, forever.

'By the way,' the fellow said, 'would you be able

to verify another name for this?' He waved the boat hook. 'A gaff, is it not? The historical record is not entirely clear.'

Gaffer bolted from the shed, was onto the wharf and over the side in one continuous motion. Saltwater swallowed him.

He swam about the harbour aimlessly. He broke the surface, Gudrin on shore calling him.

Sirens screeched in the distance. Only then did he pay heed to her. And dragged himself to shallow water.

She waded waist-high out to him and pulled him ashore. On the beach she wrapped her arms around him. The sirens drained into silence.

She led him back, across the marsh to her dwelling place. He felt the warmth of her hand, the strength of it, the desire that she stay with him.

That night he turned about in fitful sleep while she went in search of food. She returned with mussels and sea urchins. A bucket of lobsters.

'There's a fishery here, then?' he said in the morning.

'There's a scattered few fishermen from up the shore. They'll venture as far as the boundary. They make a catch, but nothing like what it used to be. Cod enough to keep their fish plant open.'

'This place, too, then,' Gaffer said, an anxiousness in his voice. 'What's to stop it from coming back?'

'One plant along the shore, no more. Government said there's not the fish for more. Never will be. Besides, they've got other notions for this place.' She shrugged. 'They will never say. Until the deal is done.'

'Tells you something when they put Skidder on the payroll,' he snapped.

Gudrin laughed, a quiet laugh that lingered.

The first he'd heard in a long time. Reminded him of his uncle, the times there'd be over a good story. His laughter crackling through the house. The easy fun of it all.

Gaffer smiled at the stir of memories, but equally at the turn of her head, how the fire caught her eyes. Her eyes holding to him. He knew he needed to be calmed, needed for a moment not to have the grip of Skidder at his throat.

Gudrin had boiled the lobsters in seawater. They devoured them. Sucked every last piece of meat from the shells. Cracked apart the insides and went for the scraps of meat. Ate the gills. Dug out the red-wax spawn and the thick green paste, wiped it into their mouths from the ends of their fingers. Gorged themselves.

A feed he would crave again. Her food and drink and company.

They lay against each other. She led him to the deep reaches of herself and held him there, and had him think he could hold to it forever.

Other questions nagged at him. Questions that nagged his smouldering sleep next to her. That took away the rest in it and pushed his mind out to the wilds.

He grew more restless the more strength he regained. Hold to some allotment doled out to him? Had never been his way, would never be.

Gudrin could see it and struggled for something to satisfy him. Talk was the best of it, though it ran its course and there was nothing more worth being said.

He would venture off alone, far out of her sight. Knowing they had sense of his every move. He would fire rocks at the fence to trigger the alarm, then race off in another direction, hoping to fool them, wanting to see places he had not seen since his return.

Once a patrol came within a footstep of nabbing him. He doubled back through the woods and fell into the house exhausted. Gudrin said nothing at first, and when she was about to, he snarled at her almost.

She made no attempt to hold him back. He would go again under the cover of night. He would taunt them with feral noises, fire rocks and sticks through the trees and watch them scurry together in jabbering clumps. Yet he could see the limits of his mockery, and knew, in the end, Skidder and his lackeys had kept the upper hand.

One day he knew he could take no more of mucking about, him some three-legged mongrel.

Planted himself in the open marsh in broad daylight and waited.

Skidder he wanted, he yelled at them. No one else. Face-to-face.

And it was Skidder he had, leaving his mob and their ATVs idling in a semicircle behind, ready to pounce at a flick of his arm. The black-uniformed grinning fool strolled slowly toward him. Stopped a few feet away and broadened the grin into a row of yellowed teeth.

Gaffer moved closer. Glared deeper at him with every step.

'Ah, Gaffer. A brave man.'

'And you're swine, Skidder.'

He chuckled. 'Think you're in any position to complain?'

'Who you working for?'

'Someone with money. Real money. Heard of it, have you, Gaffer?'

'Sweet-talking bucks?'

'My old man always said I was meant for more than a fishing boat.'

'Your old man—he wouldn't have the likes of you go near his boat. That's the one bit of sense he did have.'

Skidder's thick neck turned red. 'My old man had his hand out to the government half the time. Not me. I pay my own way, Gaffie boy. Know your trouble? You're living in the goddamn past. And haven't got the guts to face up to it.'

'You're a bloody rogue, Skidder. No better than the other bloody rogues ...'

'And you're the saviour! The saviour willing to go down with the sinking ship.'

'Get out of here! All of you!' Gaffer shouted, slinging his arm through the air.

Skidder laughed. Bloody hyena. The others revved their motors. Drooling for the kill.

Skidder held them back. He advanced, one slow step at a time. Until his face was within six inches of Gaffer's. 'This Cove is private property!'

Gaffer reached out his two hands and collared the bloodsucker. Like his father would have done, and his father before that. Up fist and nailed the bastard.

Laid him out a cold junk on the ground.

The ATVs spit dirt.

Gaffer flew away from them. Went for the salt-water.

Jumped the cliff and sailed straight down. Caught the high tide. Cut the water and never surfaced.

Skidder and his freak-friends sputtered on the bank, weapons at the hip, ready to annihilate anything that moved.

1614

Gaffer had not felt such freedom before. The sea-water swept over his creased and wounded spirit. Cleansed it. Gave back to him pride in that alloy of land and sea. Still his Island home.

He swam away, but would never clear it from his head. He swam in circles among the Virgin Rocks, reluctant to take that final lunge into the open ocean.

Cod eyed his moves, bewildered by the indecision, thinking him a strange and high-strung creature, and uncommonly timid for these parts. They were king here after all, and left to go about their business. How odd was he to act like something was forever in pursuit of him.

There was loose talk among the offshore crowd of more and bigger ships making for the Island, and word had come from down the shore of bays lined off with nets. But nothing to worry about, no reason to hole up, without the sense born and bred in them.

'You're a nervous sort. Not from around here?'

'Could be.'

'We've all come from somewhere else, one time or another, if you go far enough back.'

'Suppose so,' Gaffer said, without much interest in talk.

The wise one looked Gaffer up and down. 'Have I got any more right to this place than you? Not trying to be cocky, now. 'Tis an honest question.'

Gaffer had no answer. 'What's going to happen when that crowd and their gear show up from down the shore?'

'Drove out of it, that's what we'll be. Find another place.' The fellow turned away. With a flick that said it was not something that ever caused him worry.

Had a final word before he left. 'Always got to be ready to move on. Cause for sure and certain as soon as you find some peace and quiet something comes along to fool it up.'

Gaffer watched him go. Nothing more to do but go himself. He rose to the surface for a last look at the Cove.

Gaffer saw the girl, in the rock curve of grotto, her look fixed out to sea. Seated, arms wound around herself. Not moving. Some immutable statue.

He was about to dive away when a voice called from above him.

'Ye be havin' a gawk?'

Gaffer threw back his head to see who it could be.

'She be a fair sight, lad?'

It was Buckley, the old goat.

'She waits. For a man home from the sea, I'd be thinking.' He eyed Gaffer, smirk between chaws on the grass.

'That so,' said Gaffer. 'What's it to you?'

'Passes the time,' the old fellow said. 'Heaven knows I got lots o' time.'

Gaffer could see the glint of wisdom in his eyes. Or what passed for wisdom. He wouldn't trust it.

'I was a young buck meself one time.' Buckley grinned, head up, aiming to look particularly robust. 'I had me share of wild sprees. You might not think it, young Gaffer, but I didn't get me sense from standing still.'

'That got something to do with me?' Gaffer grunted.

'She was one of the first to come to this place,' Buckley said. His head jerked toward the shore. 'You wouldn't want her to be the last.'

Gaffer spit out a mouthful of saltwater.

'Fed up with it, are ya, me lad? Haven't got the guts for it any more?'

Gaffer glared at him. No more than a snarly, defiant glare.

'You're up against big odds. And, give the devil hes due, you put up a good fight,' Buckley said. Then snorted. Uncommonly sharp snort.

It riled Gaffer even more. He rose out of the water. 'What more?' he roared. 'Have me perish, would you? Throw me to the bloods-o'-bitches?'

'Gullshit! Grant me more sense than that.'

He fell back into the water. 'Teach me.' He mocked him. 'Wise and bearded one.'

Buckley hoofed the ground. 'Always the cynic. Must come with the place.' He shook his head.

'Well.'

'Could do with a few lessons in patience to start.' Buckley shook his head again. Then tossed it in the direction of the open sea. 'There. Look. Have a gawk.'

Sailing toward them was a three-master. Square-sail warship. Shining golden yellow in the sun, banks of guns mounted fore and aft.

'Mainwaring.'

'Pirate. Sea wolf?'

'His ship be *The Princess*. Dandiest vessel on the seven seas. Them guns would go broadside to anything afloat.'

'Why's he heading to the Island?'

'Men he wants. Crews to man his ships. You game for it? You're a stalwart lad.'

'Not me.'

'Turn cutthroat. Have at the world with cannons rammed full o' powder. You wouldn't be long having it your way.'

The notion lay open in Gaffer's head.

The ship had dropped anchor, furled its sails. Toward them, in the ship's jolly-boat came two men.

Had he wanted to escape, Gaffer would have sunk below the waves. He hauled himself on shore and stood with Buckley, their eyes not moving from the sight before them.

In the bow stood Mainwaring—spruce, sanguine, with the bearing of an educated man. No sea scum. Well-fitting doublet, lace touch of the genteel.

'Oxford man,' said Buckley. 'Not your common rogue. Still, I wouldn't cross him. Wouldn't pay to run afoul of him, especially any poor beggar what got Spanish blood coursing his veins.'

Buckley chewed his way out of sight, leaving Gaffer to deal with him.

The oarsman ran the boat onto the shifting beach rocks. Mainwaring jumped over the side and splashed the final few feet to shore.

He met Gaffer with a broad and eager smile. 'Just the strapping young pauper I've been looking for. Strong. That's certain. And backbone aplenty. Join our ship and you'll have no regrets that gold won't cure.' He laughed.

'I'll not be taking part in any thievery, if that's your game.'

He laughed again. 'Only reclaiming what is rightfully ours. Would not you do the same?'

Gaffer stood silent.

'Spaniards could do with someone to set them straight. Agreed, lad?'

Gaffer was tempted, but showed no interest.

'And what's your future, then? A fisherman, is it?'

'So be my intention.'

'Every isle must have its fishermen. And every isle must have its men to fend off those who would plunder it. I give you the choice. You're a clever fellow. You decide. Maybe one is not to be had without the other.' Yet the rogue in him could not stand still. His head rose with a curious sobriety, denoting an acclaimed station in life. An air of the noble took hold and the silent look he bestowed on Gaffer said he would be a fool not to follow him.

And neither could he silence his tongue. 'Come along, then, my lad. One look at you and I could tell you have the seafarer's soul. Not many would tempt the wrath of this crew of mine and expect to tell the tale.'

Still Gaffer would not agree to go.

Mainwaring laughed uproariously. 'You're a damn brave bugger, I grant you that. Heave yourself aboard this jolly-boat, then. We go ashore in that cove.'

Gaffer turned back to Buckley for advice, but the old fellow was long gone, no mind for anything but the path ahead. Gaffer took hesitantly to the boat and was off with a stiff thump to the back from the pirate chief, and a vacant black-tooth grin from his trusty dregs at the oars.

The jolly-boat headed for the empty cove. Not a soul to be seen. Not a house or shed, wharf or flake.

Spruce and pine and fir swept down from the hills, thinning to the headlands, its outcrops of barren rock above the splash of sea. In the shelter on the inner reaches of the cove the boat struck sand. Gaffer was the first to step ashore.

'—Tis a glorious place,' heralded Gaffer.

'Indeed it is,' said Mainwaring, looking all around. 'On this day of the year there is no finer. What I should say if I had to live here the whole year long I do not know.' He spread his hands in the air in a grandiose manner. 'Probably I should say it is no fit place for an Englishman.'

'Bad enough these few months,' said the oarsman. 'Give me the Indies any day.'

'You be a fool, then,' said Gaffer and thought nothing of it.

The fellow glared at him, and would have pitched a fist in his face had not the captain took what Gaffer said for sport and slapped him cheerfully again on the back.

It roused Gaffer to louder claims. 'There'll be no lack of West Country blood willing to root themselves in this place. Irish, too. They'll take hold to it and make it their own.'

The oarsman scoffed. 'Papists, is it. They'll not get along, the two. They'll be at each other like dogs.'

Mainwaring found Gaffer's ardour a great curiosity. 'And what will they do if the fish vanish?'

'Starve to death,' said the oarsman. 'Rot in some frozen heathen hole.'

'Swine.'

'I should think,' said Mainwaring, stepping between them, 'you'd be better to come with me. You'll like the smell of Spanish gold.'

'I'd like it well enough,' said Gaffer, 'but no gold is enough to make me forsake this place.'

The oarsman laughed. 'Drag the stunned bastard out of his misery.'

Captain was thinking just that. He was not used to such gall. A crew he had to put together and there'd be a long voyage ahead. It would not do him good to stand for it.

Yet he could not but admire the fellow, stubborn young lout that he was. Odd sort to latch on to this place as if it would come to something.

Gaffer stood his ground. Showed no sign of

bending his will, though he was not without fear of what the pirate might do. The oarsman snorted in disgust.

Captain, arms folded, bestowed on him a benevolent smile. 'Then I wish you well,' he said.

The oarsman's face fell.

And rose again in fright. Out of the corner of his eye he saw men and women, at the forest's edge, straight as the spruce. Sparsely clothed, their flesh smeared red. Some held bows. Arrows loose at the side.

'The savages,' whispered the oarsman.

Mainwaring swerved his head to them. His eyes widened. He did not speak, but moved his right hand slowly until it came to rest on his pistol.

Gaffer stiffened at the sight of them. Red ochre covering their flesh. As if they grew from the earth.

They stood unmoving. Equally startled.

One raised a hand. A fish shone silver in the sunlight.

'Do not trust them,' hissed the oarsman. 'Thieving red bastards. I heard stories—they steal whatever they can get. Have it in their heads they own this Island.'

'They would share it,' retorted Gaffer. 'You are not blind. Can you not see that?'

'Turn your back and they would slit your throat.'

'Damn the mouth on you.'

Captain glared at them. 'Enough, or I'll have my hands around both your bloody necks.'

He started toward the woods. Gaffer and the oarsman followed, kept his pace, stride for stride.

The Red Ochre whispered anxiously among themselves. Some offered weak and cautious smiles. Some held more firmly to their weapons.

Mainwaring marked his stride with a brazen confidence. 'I have heard stories of these savages. In London they are a great curiosity. Some have said they are not human. Look at them. I declare they are human. There can be no doubt about that, yet they are not at all like us. I should like one to examine at close hand.'

Gaffer saw the fervour in his eyes as he drew closer to the band. Saw his fingers never far from his pistol, his smile as he removed his hat. As he stood smartly before them, with a refined and civil bow.

He gestured to one of them, a restless young man of thick muscle and vacant eyes. The fellow quickly looked to the eldest among them. With his consent, stepped forward.

The captain met his move with a nod of respect to the elder. Turned his attention to the young man, now at his arm's length. Smiled broadly at him. Then proceeded to look him up and down. 'Very fine in stature. Extraordinary.'

The Red Ochre talked among themselves in their own urgent tongue.

'Unlike anything ever heard by Englishmen. Yet they understand each other well enough.'

Mainwaring ran a finger along the fellow's arm, from elbow to wrist. Then pulled the finger back to examine it. Smeared red. He held it to his nose.

They looked at the captain with great severity.

Still he surveyed the fellow. Now his skin clothes. Scrutinized the bone pieces hanging among the fringes.

'Curious. What do they mean?' As if the fellow would know what he had said.

The people murmured in protest.

Mainwaring drew his pistol and held it at his side.

They seemed not to know what it could do. Gaffer denounced the sight of it. 'Let them be. You have no quarrel with them.'

'I merely wish His Majesty to have the honour of seeing this fellow.' Mainwaring motioned to the oarsman. 'The Royal Court would hold it in great interest. It could do nothing but bring favour on my further voyages.'

The oarsman sprang upon the fellow. At the same moment Mainwaring fired his pistol in the air. The Red Ochre recoiled in terror.

'No harm will come to him,' Mainwaring shouted, as if shouting would make them understand. 'This man will be well taken care of. Go back to your woods and declare that you will be known to all the world.'

Gaffer went for the gun, catching the pirate unprepared. The pistol flew from his hand.

The oarsman jumped away from his captive, hauled out his own pistol with one hand, flung his sword high into the air with the other.

Gaffer was no match for them both. It was a welcome and thirsty arrow that pierced the oarsman's spine, the head of it bursting through his chest. He collapsed, lead onto the sand.

In the mêlée Mainwaring fled. Raced, a madman over the sand to the boat. Rowed toward his ship, demon loose from hell.

The man he had wanted for his trophy could have sunk an arrow in the savage of a buccaneer, but Gaffer held the fellow back. He understood that beneath the strange dress and shifting eyes there was a piece of man.

They gestured for Gaffer to come with them, join them at their summer camp. Honoured he was, and curious, but he knew he must not stay.

He left with a nod of goodwill between them. They stood on shore, guardians of the land, and watched as he walked into the saltwater. They seemed not to think it odd.

He turned with a final wave farewell, knowing they would not be people of this Island for many years more.

They watched as he dove for the last time and smiled in the knowledge that he was safe.

2041

He proposed to arrive under the cover of darkness. Yet the light coming from the surface made it brighter than midday. His head broke into air convulsed by a thunderous chain of fireworks.

The Island could never have seen such a display before.

He hardly recognized his landscape. It glittered. A maze of lights swirling from shoreline to the distant rhinestone hills. Circling a gigantic throb of neon.

What had been wharves was now a marina. To it tied sleek pleasure craft—*Paradise Café, Autumnal*

Joy, Hell or High Water. On their decks, boisterous brigades in glaring leisure suits, sucking down black rum and vodka.

'Never again!' came their shouts.

'Hydro power to the people!'

'And have-not shall be no more!'

This eruption of coloured light, was it a prize regained? Gaffer floated in the glare of it. Could comprehend not what it meant for his Island.

He swam along the shore. The marina gave way to a strip of beach. Beachfront properties—high, stilted, pre-weathered boxes—strung behind it. Revellers bursting their balconies for the best view of the sky.

Gaffer merged into the commotion of night swimmers. He brushed past a trio of naked lovers and stole ashore. No one paid him attention. Except a boozed-up guard who slurred out crap about a passport, before staggering on, drink in hand.

Gaffer untangled his way through the crowd and across the sand to a gate. Another guard looked him up and down. Gaffer recognized the wild-eyed youth in him. Knew for sure by the drug hole burning his brain.

The fellow unlatched the gate and let him in. 'Mr. Skidder will be blown away,' he hooted, snatching a phone from his belt.

Skidder was not long tracking him down. Gaffer had barely made it from the gate to Main Street when Skidder stepped out of a spotless white convertible. Himself suited up in white. Silk bow-tie. The same demented smile. New teeth.

'At last, Mr. Gaffer. I knew you would return sooner or later. You couldn't have picked a better time.'

'Who's flunkey are you now?'

'Such disrespect. You'll learn. In time. I remember you when you were a piss-ass beach crawler. Some of us never change, I'm afraid.'

'Scum.'

'Outmoded, would you not say? You're never too old to learn. Hop in, the chauffeur and I will show you around.'

The chauffeur held the door open for Gaffer. His face was set in a permanent smile.

Gaffer reluctantly agreed. No way to escape to anywhere. No place that wasn't penetrated by light.

The Cove was a theme park, Skidder its dictator of operations.

'Newfoundisney. Newfland North. Call it what you will,' said Skidder. 'But call it a success. A fucking mega success.' He spread his lips to demonstrate his row of perfect ceramic teeth.

Gaffer sat silent. Not the satisfaction of his reaction would Skidder get. At times Gaffer closed his eyes. With every hope in hell it couldn't get any worse.

'We have preserved the history of the place, of course. In fact, this original dwelling has proved to be one of our most popular exhibitions.'

Skidder spewed out his enthusiasm. Had the driver take a slow circle around Gaffer's house. Exactly as Gaffer had known it, except for the plaque in the front yard. The mouse-eared Mountie at the gate. The lineup of humanity to get inside.

'It's more than a curiosity, of course. It's our heritage. And the home of the most famous hometown girl. Gal, I should say.' He apologized. 'I always mess up that line, and she's such a sweetheart, too. So down to earth.'

Skidder propped himself up in the seat. His mouth broke into a broad and seasoned grin. 'I'm sure you'll want to see her.'

The car drew up to a private parking lot in front of the park's glittering centrepiece. 'Of course our rides and Aquatic Centre are bigger in overall area, but no attraction rivals Wonderful Grand Opryland!'

Skidder led him inside, to his private box.

The audience was wild with applause.

'Just in time for the encore. She always saves her biggest hit for last.'

The wail of steel guitar. The flash of her special spotlight. And out she came in sequinned dress, of brilliant red, and white and touch of blue.

His mother's heart going out to her adoring fans. 'You've been so good to me for so many years. This one's special. It's for y'all.' And threw them a kiss.

Gaffer could not hold back the tears.

'*I left my Island for a little bit of heaven,*' she sang, '*but my Island's now heaven to me.*'

Gaffer closed his eyes and imagined her when she held him in her arms and told him all she ever wanted was to see him a happy man.

'Everyone, sing with me … *I left my Island for a little bit of heaven, but my Island's now heaven to me.'*

They loved her. Hung on every word. As if all their hopes and dreams had been captured in two lines of a song.

It was happiness she had. And hadn't she a right to it? He thought he had his answer by the time she hit the final note and waved to them all, pulled herself off the stage.

'Goodnight, friends. Goodnight, my little Gaffer, wherever you may be.' She blew a kiss. The audience roared with applause. The stage went black. The house lights came up.

'That's her trademark exit,' said Skidder. 'Sweet, isn't it?'

Gaffer raced away, down the stairs. Tore past the security guards, into her gold-star dressing room.

His mother fell into his arms. She cried and hugged and scolded.

And when their embrace came finally to an end, Gaffer stood back, peering into his mother's eyes. Surely, beneath that make-up and diamond sheen, was a woman with regrets and pain, a longing for her other life.

It was not there to be seen. She was every inch the country queen, the hurtin' all a part of it.

Chuck had stood by his woman all these years. 'Chuck is my rock, Gaffer. He's my harbour in the storm.'

Chuck had grown no less modest. No less doting over his woman. He shone in her starlight. 'This little woman made it to the top. You be proud of her, ya hear, 'cause it ain't come easy. Right, hon? No, by God. From fish plant to fantasyland, I call it. And there's not a night goes by that she doesn't think of you, Gaffer, and pray that God has kept you safe. She even wrote a song about it. That song went to the top of the charts, but she meant every word, and then some.'

She embraced Gaffer again, a love coated in buxom glamour. She squeezed him harder than his grandmother ever did. He could only believe his mother lurked under there.

For now he kissed her gently on the cheek and wished her happiness. He shook the hand of Chuck and told him to treat her well, or he would kick his ass. The old boy guffawed and slapped his hand in Gaffer's. Shook the hell out of it.

As he was going out the door, his mother broke into song. *'Gaffer, dear, dear Gaffer, may your seas be calm, when again you are gone, dear and gentle son ...'* A tear trickled down her cheek.

'Cut!' came a call from a corner of the dressing room. 'Perfect. We'll use it in the next video.' In the bright lights, Gaffer had not noticed the video camera. 'You were great,' the face behind it called.

But Gaffer was gone like hell's flames. Skidder chasing after him.

Tearing through the crowds, weaving a route to get Skidder off his tail. Circled what had been the woods, was now a death-defying ride—The Giant Squid—through the midst of a Red Ochre ceremony at a reconstructed site.

Desperate to find Gudrin. He took his bearings at the edge of the cliffs and headed inland. The marsh was there, boardwalk across it. Led to her place. That place dwarfed by the dome of an interpretation centre.

Gaffer approached it cautiously. 'Home of the first known to this Island,' he read. 'It is said her spirit has never left.'

'Gudrin,' he called.

The tourists shook their heads at his display of emotion, tittered at his uncivilized manner. Officials shushed him with a stiff grip on his shoulder and a mouthful of urgent talk. 'Sir, you are standing on sacred ground. Please, respect the memory of their ancestral home.'

'Gudrin!' he called at the top of his lungs.

From her dwelling she emerged. The same girl, tuft of fair hair. The tourists thought her someone there to play a part and despaired at the intimacy between them.

Gaffer hurried her away. The tourists moaned after them and shook their fists and cried foul. Demanded a refund. Declared it nothing but a sham and went back to riding their fantasies under the flash of fireworks.

The two were running now. A place where no one would find them? Gudrin knew such a place, hole in the wall of the cliff. She guided him down a narrow path. They clung to each other. Held on, the only two on the Island who remembered it.

Knew they would not give in. Even at the sound of Skidder high over them, his searchlights sweeping down the cliff.

'Gaffie boy!' Regressed to his demented call. 'What goes down must come up.'

The pair slipped into the hole, foiled his light.

Skidder perched on the crag then. Eagle waiting out his prey, his talons fearsome, razor hooks; his smirk seething, goddamnable.

The curious, the bloodthirsty, trickled in behind him, video cameras at the hip, hoping for the worst, ready to auction the footage, to hold out for their millions.

The two ragged souls fell together, weary for the world that was their own. Gudrin held his face in her hands and kissed and kissed his twisted mouth. She held his head to her chest, murmured words of who he would always be.

His rage passed to a rasp grinding the night air, rock against rock shifted by the sea. His words the sound of that rock, the splash on that rock, the swallowing of the sea.

He caught her eyes in the flash of light. Would not have her think all faith had fallen from him. He felt her breath against his face. And knew a greater sigh that filled the heavens. That put their fireworks to shame.

Together they breathed in the moon and the stars. Slept amid God.

It was the crackle of his mind that woke him. He kissed her sleep. She did not stir, and he set his mind to imagining other fates that might wash ashore.

Above him circled the frenzied hordes gnawing at the rocks. Clamouring in the name of common good, each for a piece of the show. Skidder held them at bay, a mongrel at his best. The glory of the kill was not for sharing.

The wind rose. Salt air, blood of his Island, blew in his face. Salt spray, the fisherman's balm, drove up from the rocks below. Soused his flesh. Saltwater sweat streamed in rivers across the rock of his face. His father's will, grip on his own grandfather's gaff, rose in him, salt of his youth.

His eyes narrowed, wrinkled with the stir of his heart. Expectation curved his lips. The edge of a smile that none, save the creatures of the sea, could know.

What was to become of him, of her, their swell of an island?

She stirred with the wind. Together they charmed the night air with their schemes.

Overhead, the gamegear assembled, their helicopters hovered, ropes and nooses dangling from the hatches. Screaming white light hellbent for the hole in the wall.

Bullhorns blaring orders. 'Grab the ropes. Clamp the harness around you. Now!' They relished the combat zone.

When the enemy did not show themselves the troops blared all the louder. 'Bloody fools. Die, die, you will, if you can make no more claim to sense than this.'

They came into the glare in their own good time. Upright, strong-bodied as ever. Hanging tough as sod to the rocks. They planted themselves there. Not to move an inch but of their own accord.

'You sleeveens,' Gaffer yelled. 'Rock slime!'

The pair inched forward to the very edge of the crag, hand tight in hand. Raising free hands through the air.

The rescue ropes snaked before their faces. More maniac copter blades chomped the air in a deafening whirr, news crews sparring for the choicest spot. The edge of the cliff above mounded with bodies and their machines, every eye through a lens, every forefinger on the video triggers.

'No use!' came Skidder's roar, louder than all the rest. 'Surrender. This will make you rich. TV. Movies. Endorsements. You'll never have to work again.'

Their free hands curled to fists. Their faces a dogged wild unflinching twist. Fate, their own to unfurl.

When the frenzy had reached its shrillest pitch, they bent forward, homage to the broad Atlantic. Slowly raised their heels, feet clenching the rock.

And sprang from this Island! This brace of abiding souls thrust into the salted air. Seabirds to soar, and plunge down the face of the cliff. Into the black and seething waters.

The masses bellowed their disappointment. No rescue. The package deal had promised them a thrill a minute.

Skidder cast his finger at the sea. At the sweep of searchlight there. 'Look. Quick! There's one of them. Take to the boats. You've not had the last of it. You'll not go home empty-handed. You'll have your footage yet by hell.'

By hell they did. Every boat blocked to the gunwales. Every last one of them, except his mother, in pursuit. A massive flotilla out the Cove with the crack of dawn.

Gudrin had struck the water and was gone her own way.

Gaffer left to lure them on. Backstroking it through

the water, looking back at them. Plunging under for minutes at a time, only to shoot out of the water, dolphin from the best Marineland they had ever seen.

He gave them quite the wicked show. Race and roll; arch, flip and fold. Aquatics such as the folks had never witnessed before. They stood on the decks and applauded. Going to second and third video discs, applauding the potential for money if they could only capture him.

Each time they drew close, Gaffer dove away with a triumphant, effervescent wave.

'After him!' Again, but no closer to their goal.

All the time farther and farther out to sea.

'These fishing banks are grand, you say!' Gaffer yelled. 'Salt with the sweat of hundreds and thousands of crews. Salt with the death of a good many of them. You're on sacred ground, you crowd!'

It did nothing to slow their pursuit. Ravenous hounds. They could smell the greenbacks. The air was rife with it.

Their boats barely skimmed the water. The speed of the chase fired their blood anew. 'More, more!'

More thrills than whitewater rafting. More history in the making.

'Beneath these waves, the wreck of that Island lies. Lies like sunken nets. Hulls ripped abroad, a toppled rig ... The Island's a mirage now, bloodsuckers! Suck the carrion dry.'

They relished his passion. Delighted in the way his voice soared above the waves, over the wind.

They did not notice the rising of the wind. Or did not care. Or had the technology to outrun it.

Or so they thought.

Gaffer lured them farther and farther off the shore. Into the brunt of a hurricane's tail sweeping up the seaboard.

From the calm beneath the waves he watched the wind pitch and sling their boats.

And heave every last body overboard. Every last one of them to their briny end. Amen.

1497

The waters surrounding the Island ran thick and fast. Evolution had loaded the sea with fish, driven the multitudes past the capes, tucked them into every bay and cove.

Capelin spewed onto empty beaches, eggs and milt swirled together in a teeming, fertile stew. Threw themselves back out to sea, food for the cod. Cod food for the seals. Chain unending.

Gaffer gloried in their numbers. He fused with the swarms, let himself be borne by the thick of cod, carried along by the undulating mass that swam with grace and pride and regency.

'We are called king cod for good reason,' said one. 'We rule this coast by God, and that ever shall be, and he who thinks otherwise is brainless as a herring.'

Gaffer embraced their cockiness, took a dose of it for himself. Circled the Island, a warrior marking territory. Thrust himself through the saltwater, demon-eyed, lusting to stake claim for generations to come. That none but the fair and decent should ever land upon its shores.

He cut the surface fancy and free, nothing to temper his wild display. Not a boat, not a foreign ripple had ever found its way to shore. Gaffer lay naked on his back and soaked in the sun's rays, the smell of pine wafting from the hills.

'Gaffer.'

He flipped onto his stomach. Saw Gudrin tread-ing the water nearby. The sunlight catching the wet marvel of her face, a sparkling gauze.

'You forget I have been here long ago,' she said. 'The Red Ochre even longer. And others before them. You are not king after all.' She chuckled.

'I did not forget.'

He took to the water, waist-deep. She swam toward him. Stood up and wiped the water from her eyes.

He embraced her without pause. And she him. They clung to each other, swayed exultant in the saltwater. Hands madly groping each other in the reflection of the wild woods, uncharted shores.

Lovers they were. Wild, frenzied lovers of a thousand years. Upon the tidal sand; raw revelry with capelin lapping over them. Waves burying them, receding then. Again and again. Lovers of the sea, lovers of the land.

And from the woods came the eyes of red faces. Eyes that crinkled at the sight of the pair. Smiles buried in the trees.

In the afterglow Gaffer glimpsed a faint square of mast on the horizon.

Pierced the spell. Nagged at him until he floated away from the landwash.

Toward the ship, Gudrin his equal in the swim. The two pushed out to sea, called to confront the full measure of the ship. To witness the turn of history.

They left the natives of the woods to wonder at the same far-distant sight, and draw back at the thought of such a vessel coming to their shores.

The pair of swimmers lunged on, bodies curled together, now beneath the waves. His mouth lingering against hers when she had need of air.

They rose to the surface as past them plunged the ship's anchor. Rose to the cries of twenty men feasting on the sight of land.

'No eyes ever laid on it before!'

'Done us proud, that you have, Caboto!'

Every eye gazing at cliffs that gave way to beach and the wooded hills beyond. And not one man could get his fill.

Until Gudrin's voice rang at them. 'Yours not the first pair of eyes, Caboto! Go home, Venetian. Get back to Bristol. There's nothing for you to claim.'

Stunned they were. Too stunned to heed a word.

'Look! Heathens! Creatures never seen by man.'

'By the grace of God, in the name of the King of England ... what isles have we reached?'

Gudrin shouted again, 'None that has any need of your infernal greed!'

They paid no mind. 'Look at the codfish teeming in these waters.'

A crewman lowered a basket over the side of the ship, and without hook or bait, hauled to deck several lusty cod.

'The markets will never want for fish again.'

Gaffer railed at their bloody intentions.

All on deaf ears. They took to the ship's boat and rowed to shore. Ignoring their detractors, leaving them to flail the water in useless anger.

Caboto at the prow, eyes narrowed to the beach, his plumed hat angled as if God had placed it there. His foot forward against the gunwale, its motion to signal the beginning of the Island's history.

He set that foot to land and the sand yielded to him. The forests fell silent. Its dwellers cared not for the impatient splash of his step. Their eyes set upon him. Him and his parade of men that struck the shore.

They planted there a cross, a banner to the King, another to the Pope. They declared the land their own. Crossed themselves and promptly headed to their boat again.

They had seen the remnants of a fire upon the shore. Could feel the eyes against their backs when into the boat they scrambled.

Within the shadow of their ship, they did not fail to grow loud in triumph. 'We will return. Us and a thousand ships more.'

'With your firearms, curs,' Gaffer shouted at them, hanging now onto the gunwales of their boat. 'And your nets. Scour the Island and its seas you will and think nothing of it. Damn you all.'

'Blasphemer!' they charged.

And smote the pair with the flat of their oars. Knocked them senseless. Pitched them face-first into the saltwater.

They floated there, flotsam of forthright wilful men. Colonial dross. Soon to sink to the ocean floor where all the Island's secrets are at rest.

'Salvage them. Haul them aboard. Salt them in

the hold. They'll give us eager conversation (praise God!) at the King's banquet table. And the dear Pope shall have their souls.'

They were brought to life by the blare of a harbour symphony. The surging howl of every ship's horn within a hundred miles. The relentless peal of church bells all across the land.

Gaffer and Gudrin dragged themselves from history's hold. Hauled themselves up from the bilge to deck. Into the brunt of celebration—five hundred years since Caboto's foot was set to land. They stood aboard his ship reincarnated in the year of our Lord nineteen hundred and ninety-seven.

They looked to the stern. The ship just passed the Island's hibernating marvel, its millennial masterwork, a massive oil stage being towed now out to sea. Soon to perform, to the tune of wind and waves, as the fair Island's saving grace.

How sweet the sound / That saved a wretch like me ... Gaffer's eyes shut tight.

He turned and faced the bow.

The ship sailed through a narrow channel, entry to the Island's capital. Banners flew from the highest hills, water cannons spewed the air with rainbows, politicians declared it the dawn of another era. The foghorns wailed.

Nouveau Caboto waved his hand in blessing to the throng, plumed hat held firm. Broadened his smile with every jaunty toss of his regal head. He commanded the bow, the conquering hero.

The tourists massed on shore and raved. Flung fake sou'westers in the air. Exalted the man who put this Island on the map.

Unnoticed by a single soul, save one, Gaffer's head sank into his hands.

'No good will that do us,' she said to him.

He shook his head.

'Buck up, Gaffer. Your father wouldn't want you slouched down like some slovenly vagabond.'

'What, join that lot? Put on a show for the tourists? Make out there's a job to be had?'

She hauled him up on his two feet. 'By God, bayman ...' Fire in her eyes.

He had to smile, and laugh. Loud and heretical. Like he'd never done before.

He grabbed the Island's flag and led a race with her up the rigging. Straight up. Higher and higher, over Caboto's head. As sure of foot as ever he was. Death-defying acrobats, the two. All the time the flag swirling in the wind.

They hauled themselves into the crow's-nest. Climbed atop its rails. Their free hands sweeping the flag across the sky. Its golden arrow staking claim.

Gaffer howled.

The shoreline crowds roared at their courage. Cried 'New Found Land!' Tens of thousands of them. 'New Found Land!'

Catcalled bold Caboto. Him now swearing bravely beneath his foreign breath.

The pair let go their grip on the rigging. Balanced on the rails—great auks high above the pomp and circumstance. Each gripped two corners of the flag. And leapt full-force. Sailed the air. The flag, blazoned across the sky, breaking their fall.

They swerved and arched, and did great tricks.

Landed, thanks be to God, feet-first into the water. Eyes, ears, mouths tightly shut. Arms spread wide for fear of being mired in the harbour muck.

They swam ashore, breaking water ahead of Caboto's ship.

Hauled themselves up the pier, onto dry land. Dripping saltwater as they ran. The crowds split to left and right. Up from the harbourfront, onto the streets they sprinted, arms raised high, flag rippling in the air.

Through the city streets, cheered on their way, saltwater olympians. Home from the sea. Hunters home from the hill.

The crowds thinned at the outskirts of the place, though there was always a scattered few to stand and wave. More to smile and lamely nod.

They headed home across the Island. The closer to it they came, the more they slowed, the more the flag fell limp.

At the crest of the hill that brought the green of the Cove in view, Gaffer stopped. His eyes explored the land and its own small harbour. They marvelled at its beauty.

'No wonder the first ones chose this place,' said Gudrin.

'For what good it ever did.'

'Chiselled you, didn't it?' she said, and laughed at him, and tied the flag playfully tight to his neck.

He stared for a long time at the place. Saw not much sign of life. But enough to look for more.

He turned to her. She had already begun to slip away. 'See you, will I, tomorrow, and the next day after that?'

'Your father the same? You be looking for us both,' she said. 'I hear someone calling my name.'

Gaffer stood before her to block her way.

She smiled. 'And someone calling you.'

She kissed him on the lips. Drew away.

She had not gone far when she stopped and looked back. 'It would grow old and show its years. Sometimes love is best put away. For other times.'

She was gone then, past the woods.

He started along the road again, down the hill, into the Cove. Only when he came in sight of his house did he think of anyone but her.

His mother was outside, working in the vegetable garden. She looked up. 'Where have you been, my love? I was beginning to worry.' She stood up, shielding her eyes against the sun. 'In the water?'

'Of course,' he said.

'I worry. You know I do.' She embraced him and told him he meant all the world to her.

When he drew back she pressed her hands in his. 'Be careful. You do no one any good if you don't keep a level head between those shoulders.'

'As level as ever I could.' He smiled.

They were interrupted by his grandmother billowing through the front door.

'My God, my God …' She made for him, snatched him to her, sunk him to her bosom. 'And I thought for sure you'd run off. I didn't know what to think, all that foolishness you goes on with. I said to your mother, he's gone this time for sure. We'll never hear tell of him again. Not a hide nor hair. Gone, gone, my dear, you might as well face it. The Lord got better uses for him than what we do.'

She squeezed him harder than she ever did before.

Damn near cut off his breath. 'But you're back, and I got breakfast warm in the oven, waitin' for ya.'

She jostled him into the house and to the kitchen table.

Gaffer offered no resistance. Dug into the pancakes. Ate every scrap of them, and praised his grandmother's efforts to the heavens.

'There'll be youngsters of yours yet, please God, runnin' around the yard, stuffin' their dear little faces with me pork buns.' She gave him another peck on the cheek.

Gaffer slipped away, when his grandmother had to give her swollen legs a rest. She lay down on the daybed in the kitchen, her eyes closed, her smile set permanently on her face.

He made his way down the road. Took in the air of the place. The salt sea smell, as strong as it had ever been. The air wound itself around him, penetrated to the core of him, cleared his head of all that tried to clog his brain.

Had to suck it into him, drive into his head the reason for fighting off every last scrap of their doubletalk.

He found the old fellow, sitting still on his veranda. 'Alzheimer's, me arse,' he said when he laid eyes on Gaffer.

Gaffer laughed. Had to see the sport in it.

Gaffer put it to him. 'What do you make of 'em all?'

'Who, b'y, who?'

'The government crowd.'

'Stun as me arse, half o' them.'

Gaffer laughed again.

'Some does their best, I s'pose. Say they do anyway.' The old fellow leaned forward in his chair. 'Can't go through life waiting for foreigners to make up yer mind.'

'Can't have 'em smack you down when you get up off yer arse, either.'

Now it was the old fellow who laughed.

'Look around, Gaffer. This place worth salvaging? Some future in it? What?' He leaned back. 'That's for you young crowd. I had me time.'

Gaffer gave him a nod. Strode up to him and shook his hand. Left him to his peace and quiet. Just in time to miss his slippered wife.

GAFFER

He made his way down the road, to the wharves and the beach.

The old people, and the ones not yet gone to the mainland, and the scattered few others, all came out on their front steps and watched him pass. They held up hesitant hands to him.

'You be careful, Gaffer. Need you. We do so.'

Gaffer raised a hand to them all. Showed something of the smile they were waiting for. He walked on with their blessing.

When he came to his uncle's shed he stopped. Stood there, and looked it over. He could almost hear his uncle's voice inside.

He walked on. Down to the landwash. Planted himself on the beach rocks and fixed his look out to sea.

His breath quickened. The sea bade to him, wanting him, wanting to encircle him, isolate him, protect him.

His skin tightened, toughened at the spray.

He peered through narrowing eyes to the headland. Was sure it was Buckley that he saw.

Gaffer looked behind him, along the sand bank. No one. Turned around completely. No one anywhere.

He stared back out to sea. Leaned into the spray.

From the edge of the bank grew the noise of a rusted Ford. Their hysteric laughter. Their voices out of windows.

One yelling down at him, 'Gaffer! What the fuck ya at now?'